ABOUT THE AUTHOR

Jane Peart, award-winning novelist and short story writer, grew up in Asheville, North Carolina, and was educated in New England. Although she now lives in northern California, her heart has remained in her native South—its people, its history, and its traditions. With more than twenty-five novels and 250 short stories to her credit, Jane likes to emphasize in her writing the timeless and recurring themes of family, traditional values, and a sense of place.

Ten years in the writing, the *Brides of Montclair* series is a historical, family saga of enduring beauty. In each new book, another generation comes into its own at the beautiful Montclair estate near Williamsburg, Virginia. These compelling, dramatic stories reaffirm the importance of committed love, loyalty, courage, strength of character, and abiding faith in times of triumph and tragedy, sorrow and joy.

Jubilee Bride

Book Nine
The Brides of Montclair Series

JANE PEART

ZondervanPublishingHouse
Grand Rapids, Michigan

A Division of HarperCollinsPublishers

To Anne Severance,
an editor of skill and sensitivity,
with admiration, appreciation, affection

JUBILEE BRIDE
Copyright © 1992 by Jane Peart

Requests for information should be addressed to:
Zondervan Publishing House
Grand Rapids, Michigan 49530

Library of Congress Cataloging-in-Publication Data

Peart, Jane.
    Jubilee bride / Jane Peart.
        p.   cm. – (Brides of Montclair series : bk. 9)
    ISBN 0-310-67121-3 (softcover)
    I. Title. II. Series: Peart, Jane. Brides of Montclair series :
bk. 9.
    PS3566.E238J8 + 11992
    813'.54—dc20   92–9694
                                                                CIP

Edited by Anne Severance
Interior design by Kim Koning
Cover design by Art Jacobs
Cover illustration by Wes Lowe, Sal Baracc and Assoc., Inc.

Printed in the United States of America

92 93 94 95 96 97 / LP / 10 9 8 7 6 5 4 3 2 1

A Note to My Readers

FOR NEW READERS of the the Brides of Montclair series, the following is a brief summary of the characters of this book, their background, relationships, and current status.

Faith Devlin is the daughter of Garnet Cameron (*Rebel Bride*), widowed from her first marriage to Bryson Montrose, now married to Jeremy Devlin, an American executive of a British publishing company. They live in England, dividing their time between a London town house and a country estate.

Blythe Dorman Montrose (*Gallant Bride* and *Shadow Bride*) married Rod Cameron in 1887. They live now at Cameron Hall outside of Mayfield, Virginia, with their three children— a young son, Scott, and twins, Katherine and Carmella. Blythe's son, Jeff, by her first husband, Malcolm Montrose, is a college student at Oxford in England.

Jonathan Montrose, son of Malcolm Montrose (deceased) and his first wife, Rose Meredith (*Yankee Bride*), is now the master of Montclair, the Montrose ancestral Virginia home. He and his wife, Davida Carpenter, have two children, Kendall and Meredith.

His cousin, Druscilla Montrose (*Destiny's Bride*), married Randall Bondurant, who was formerly married to their cousin, Alair Chance. As children, all three cousins grew up at Montclair. After the War Between the States, Bondurant won the family estate from Malcolm in a card game. Subsequently, Dru deeded the property back to Jonathan, as the rightful heir. The Bondurants, including Lenora and Lalage, two daughters born of Randall's union with Alair, and Dru's and Randall's own child, Evalee, now live in South Carolina, on an island plantation called Hurricane Haven.

—Jane Peart

Prologue

Oxford, England
Summer 1892

ON A GLORIOUS June morning, Jeff Montrose left his student lodgings and wheeled his bicycle from the shadowed arch into the sunshine. There he stood for a moment, listening to the musical chiming of the bells from Magdalen Chapel.

Even though he would not be among the worshipers called to the early Sunday service, Jeff felt a sense of almost religious exaltation. To his heightened senses, everything seemed more intensely beautiful this morning—the sky more blue, the sun more dazzling, giving the white hawthorn blossoms a unique iridescence and the stones of the centuries-old buildings, a silvery patina.

With the peal of the church bells still echoing in the summer air, Jeff hefted his lean, six-foot frame onto his bike and pedaled down a narrow Oxford lane toward the river.

At the riverbank Jeff leaned the bike against a tree, brushed back his dark tousled hair, and walked down to the water's edge. In a few hours the river would be choked with skiffs, canoes, and punts—flat, shallow boats favored by his romantically inclined fellow students who enjoyed propelling their ladyloves lazily downstream. But now the water was still, with hardly a ripple to mar its crystalline surface. Jeff watched it sweep by, soothing the strange excitement that had gripped his soul for the past few days.

He had returned to Oxford from London on a late train the night before and had slept deeply, exhausted from his days in the city. Awakening at dawn, he was still too stimulated, too excited to go back to sleep.

Yesterday he had remained at the exhibit until the gallery guards had been forced to remind him that it was nearly closing time, and Jeff had had to tear himself away.

He still found it hard to believe that the paintings of the pre-Raphaelite artists—Millais, Burne-Jones, and Holman Hunt—embodied so nearly his own dream pictures, images he had carried in his own imagination for years. They had been painted in such exquisite detail that he felt he could reach out and actually finger the velvet robes, touch the long, glorious wavy hair of the epic heroines, pick up the lush fruit, stroke the finely reproduced animals—the little sleeping dog, the doe with its slender legs and startled eyes—

It had been almost a spiritual experience, he thought, if the heady rush he had felt could be described as spiritual—that urgent feeling that he must paint, that he would never know true completion, true happiness until he set on canvas the dreams of his heart.

Painting was the answer to all that restlessness within him, that unsettledness that his mother and especially his stepfather, Rod Cameron, found so disturbing in him. All their suggestions for a choice of career, a plan for his future had fallen on deaf ears. He knew that subconsciously he had been listening for something else, another voice telling him: "This is the way, walk ye in it."

Jeff was almost embarrassed to employ words from Scripture for the inner conviction he had felt while gazing rapturously at the paintings. He had not been very faithful about attending church since coming to Oxford. Even when visiting his mother and Rod in Virginia on holiday, he had become lax about accompanying them to Sunday services. And only rarely did he attend the village church with the Devlins when he spent weekends at Birchfields with Aunt Garnet.

But this feeling, conviction, vision—whatever one could call it—didn't seem to have anything to do with church services. Rather, it was a sensation of deep reverence. It was an inner knowing–as if Someone had told him—that he could paint. No, it was more than that. If ever he were to become the person he was supposed to be, all that his Creator meant for him to be, he *must* paint!

The problem, Jeff realized, would be breaking the news to his mother and Rod that he was dropping out of the university, that instead of pursuing his architectural studies, he would be studying *art*. They would object, of course. Especially Rod. He would consider it—what—an unmanly profession? Well, it wouldn't be the first time Rod Cameron had disapproved of him. When staying at Cameron Hall, Jeff had always felt his stepfather's silent disapproval.

It wasn't that he disliked Rod. It was just that the two men had practically nothing in common. Rod's interest was largely confined to horses. He raised thoroughbreds and hunters. In fact, Cameron Hall was known throughout Virginia and even beyond for its fine stable. To Rod, besides his wife and three small children, nothing else in the world seemed to matter. Perhaps Rod's own son, little Scott, wouldn't disappoint him as Jeff felt that he himself had.

His mother, too, always seemed tense when he came to

visit, anxious that her son would say or do something to upset Rod. Jeff shrugged. Sometimes Jeff felt that his mere *existence* was enough to upset his stepfather. And what could he do about it? He was a living reminder to Rod that his mother had loved another man, had borne his child.

At least Rod obviously adored her. Jeff was happy about that and loved his little half brother and sisters. But Virginia wasn't home. He had come to accept that since returning to England after graduating from Brookdale Preparatory. England was home for him—not Cameron Hall in Virginia.

Besides, his godparents, Edward and Lydia Ainsley, with whom he stayed when in London, were as close as any family could be. He knew they considered him almost a son, the child they had never had. Aunt Lydia especially would be interested and supportive of his new plan. He would have to tell her soon.

Yes, he'd see his tutor tomorrow, tell him what he intended to do. He'd pack his things, find some place to live in London near the Royal Academy, see about enrolling for classes. There was a sense of relief now that he had made up his mind. He no longer felt troubled by a dozen imagined reasons why he shouldn't move on to satisfy the desire that had flamed into being after seeing the exhibit in London. He had the answer now. He knew what he had to do and how he would go about doing it.

The sun was up. He felt it warm on his back. Knowing that his solitude would soon be intruded upon, Jeff turned reluctantly from the river, got back on his bike, and rode back to his his lodgings.

Parking the bicycle in front, he took the stone steps to his upper apartment, two at a time. Unlocking his door, he went inside. On the table in the entryway, unnoticed the night before in his fatigue, he found a pile of envelopes. The top one bore a Virginia postmark and his mother's familiar handwriting. Before opening any of the other mail, Jeff tore open this one.

A bank check fell out from the folds of the stationery. Searching for some explanation, his eyes raced down the sheets of paper with its neat lines of script. The check was for passage to Virginia when the present term ended. "We are all so anxious to see you and have you here for the summer," she had written.

Jeff let out a low moan. For a moment he stood staring into space, then with a determined squaring of his shoulders he pocketed the check. He'd explain later, and they'd understand. At least, he sincerely hoped they would. But even if they didn't, it would be too late.

He sifted through the rest of his mail, saw the one from Aunt Garnet Devlin, and ripped it open. It was an invitation to Birchfields for the following weekend.

Good idea! he thought. He always enjoyed his visits in the country, and, of course, to see Faith. She was always great fun. He couldn't wait to share his plan with her. Faith always listened to him, sympathized, supported him—no matter what.

And after the weekend . . . then his adventure would really begin.

Part I
The Adventure Begins

England
Summer 1892

Man's love is of man's life a thing apart,
'Tis woman's whole existence.

—Lord Byron

chapter

1

Birchfields
The Devlins' Country Home
Outside London, England

THE DINING ROOM at Birchfields was perhaps Garnet's favorite in all the large Tudor mansion. On this mild summer evening the French windows stood open, admitting a soft breeze fragrant with flowers from the garden. The long table set with the new china service gleamed in the glow of tall, lighted tapers in twisted silver candelabra, and the centerpiece of white tulips and blue delphinium pleased her especially.

The menu, too, was superb—the jellied soup, the fresh sole in cream sauce, the *petit pois*, and parsleyed potatoes. Tomorrow she must be sure to compliment the cook.

Her seating plan had been inspired, Garnet observed. Placing the young people on both sides of the table opposite each other and interspersing them with the rather staid older couples—the Edgertons, Jeremy's publisher and his wife, and the Vicar and Mrs. Bentley-Todd—had kept things lively. Even the vicar was laughing heartily at some amusing comment of Tom's.

Yes, the entire weekend is going very well, she thought with satisfaction.

Garnet's gaze roamed the length of the table, then lingered a moment longer on her daughter. Faith seemed to be enjoying herself tonight. She often didn't. Why the girl did not seem to derive much pleasure from social occasions, Garnet could not for the life of her understand. Her own life as a belle had been such fun, that is, until that dreadful War had come along and the love of her life, Malcolm Montrose, had brought home his Yankee bride!

A burst of laughter brought Garnet back to the present, annoyed that she had not caught the remark that had prompted it.

Although she tried to keep her mind on the flow of conversation during the dessert of fruit sorbet, Garnet subconsciously kept track of Neil Blanding. In her opinion, with his blond Viking good looks and courtly manners, his pleasant personality and keen intelligence, Neil would be an ideal husband for Faith. Not only that, his background and breeding were impeccable. Bearing one of the oldest names in the county, his family was among the wealthiest landowners. Furthermore, Neil was in line for a title through his father's bachelor brother, Lord Blanding. Yes, in every way, Neil was Faith's best possibility for a prestigious marriage . . . *if* the foolish girl would only realize it!

At the moment, however, Neil was involved in an animated conversation with pretty Lady Allison Ashford, who would be presented at Court with Faith later this summer. Garnet felt a pinch of irritation and frowned. Why wasn't Faith paying attention? Then, remembering that ladies over forty must take care not to cause any more lines than possible, Garnet quickly smoothed her brow.

It was Allison's aunt, Lydia Ainsley, who was sponsoring

Faith's presentation at Court. In fact, it was through Lydia's friendship with Blythe Montrose, now Garnet's sister-in-law, that this honor was being bestowed on Faith. Bother! Why did she have to think about Blythe now!

Garnet knew that her old resentment of Blythe Montrose Cameron should have long since disappeared, especially since her marriage to Garnet's brother had given Rod at last this long-awaited happiness. But deep down she had to admit that it still rankled. After all, if Malcolm Montrose, Garnet's first love, had not met and married Blythe in California, he might have come home to *her!*

Determinedly she directed her gaze to her husband, Jeremy Devlin—kind, patient, considerate. Hadn't he rescued her from a life of poverty and deprivation after the War and given her, instead, everything she had lost and more? When she realized he was looking at her with a kind of questioning in his gray eyes, she favored him with one of her most dazzling smiles.

Jeremy felt a familiar sensation in his heart as he returned his wife's smile. He had never ceased to be amazed at his own good fortune in persuading this woman to marry him. He often saw that confirmed in the admiring looks of other men as they followed her slim figure with their eyes, listened to her laugh, were captivated by her charm—

Garnet might not be considered beautiful, he knew, but she had something far more valuable than mere beauty. *She has a look that is distinctly her own*, he mused. Her graceful carriage in the clothes she could now afford gave her a stunning appearance. And if there were a single gray hair in her reddish-blond hair, it had been dispensed with or skillfully disguised. The final effect was one in which Jeremy had always taken great pride. Yes, he was a lucky man indeed.

Still, he knew, his wife could be manipulative, trying to

maneuver people and events her way. Right now, noticing the tiny pucker on Garnet's forehead, he wondered just what she might be up to, and following her glance, saw that their daughter was listening with rapt attention to whatever Jeff Montrose was saying, while Neil Blanding and the young Ashford girl were chatting. So, that was it. Garnet was concerned about Faith's prospects, and Lady Allison posed a threat. He hoped Garnet wouldn't interfere. More than anything in the world, Jeremy wanted his daughter's happiness, and whichever young man would make her happy—

Neil Blanding, having completed the inconsequential exchange with Allison, found his gaze traveling automatically to Faith Devlin. How lovely she looked in the candlelight. Her cheeks were flushed, her eyes sparkling, her lips curved in an enchanting smile. Her whole face was alive and radiant. Maybe it had something to do with Jeff Montrose, who had monopolized her the whole evening, he thought with a flicker of irritation.

Neil felt a pang that was part jealousy, part discouragement. He had known since it had been drummed into him as a teenager that it was his duty as the only son of his family to marry and continue the distinguished line, to ensure the title. He had assumed that his bride would come from the dozen or so young women in the small circle of titled families in his class.

But instead of one of the young ladies his mother, Lady Ellen, might have picked out for him, Neil had met Faith Devlin. She was not only of American parentage but possessed all the characteristics and personality traits his mother deplored. She was outspoken, opinionated, independent and . . . Neil was completed fascinated with her! Of all the young women he knew, Faith was the only one he wanted.

Although she had told him over and over it was hopeless, Neil had a stubborn streak as well, and he continued to hope that one day she might change her mind.

Faith, suddenly conscious of Neil's adoring eyes upon her, felt a rush of sympathy. Dear Neil. She wished he would find someone right for him, someone as accomplished and affectionate as he deserved. Maybe then he would stop clinging to the possibility that she might come to care for him. Of course, she *did* care for him, but he wanted more. He wanted the kind of love she could give only Jeff.

Faith experienced a twinge in her own heart. Was she, too, holding on to an impossible dream?

Feeling Faith's eyes on him, Jeff realized that there had not yet been a chance for them to talk, no opportunity to tell her about his plan. Ever since his arrival at Birchfields, there had been only a press of people and fast-paced activity. He was bursting to tell someone, especially Faith. He could always count on her to back up his belief in himself and his dreams.

What an interesting face she has, he thought, watching her in animated conversation with her guests. *The high cheekbones, the dark wings of brows, the hair swept simply back from her forehead, her clear hazel eyes. Is it her eyes that make her so . . . well, yes . . . so beautiful?*

Someday he must paint Faith, Jeff decided. Someday when he really knew how to do her justice. Tomorrow he'd have to find a way to get her off somewhere alone. Then he'd share everything with her.

"I know what you mean," Faith was saying, nodding her head. "Let me share a family joke!" She threw Garnet a mischievous look. "I once overheard this exchange between my mother and one of the foreign guests Papa had brought down for the weekend. The gentleman said politely to Mama, 'Mrs. Devlin, I understand you are an American.' To which

Mama replied—" Here Faith's eyes danced wickedly as she paused to deliver the *coup de grace*. With another teasing look at her mother, Faith, in an exact imitation of Garnet's soft Southern accent, finished, " 'Why no, suh. I am a *Virginian!* "

There was a peal of delighted laughter. Even Garnet joined in good-naturedly. This story, which had been told on her dozens of times, always provoked great hilarity. As long as her guests were entertained, it didn't disturb her one whit to be the butt of a joke told in good taste.

"Virginians are a rare breed," Jeff murmured in acknowledgment. "With apologies to you, of course, Aunt Garnet."

Faith giggled. "Virginians worship their ancestors, just as the Chinese do."

"No more than the English, I'm afraid. Right, Allison?" suggested Neil with a glance at Lady Allison.

What a nice sense of humor Neil has, Garnet thought approvingly. *A rare trait for an Englishman.* She glanced over at her daughter, hoping that Faith appreciated that aspect of his personality, too.

It was then that Garnet saw Faith and Jeff exchanging a look, their eyes locking for a long moment. Garnet felt a sharp little dart of alarm. Even after Jeff had turned away, she could see the expression on Faith's face. It was one Garnet recognized only too well.

It can't be! It must have been the gleam of candlelight, she told herself, trying her best to dismiss the thought. *It's only a trick of the light*—but in her heart, she knew better.

chapter

2

GARNET STEPPED out onto the terrace, thinking how lovely the grounds looked on this summer afternoon. From the terrace, ringed with pottery urns spilling red and salmon-pink geraniums, she could survey the gardens, splendid with masses of blue and purple delphiniums, coral and magenta snapdragons, white alyssum and yellow daylilies. Under her direction the gardens here had come alive. She had taken great pains to fashion them after those at Cameron Hall, her beloved childhood home in Virginia.

Looking cool in a lemon-yellow India silk gown, its simple design belying its cost, she stood for a moment at the edge of the stone steps before opening a parasol made of matching silk and moving gracefully down onto the velvety lawn to inspect the tables set for tea.

Under a leafy canopy of oaks, white wicker chairs, plump with cushions of flowered chintz, encircled a round table covered with a hand-drawn pink linen cloth and napkins. Garnet scrutinized the table setting, then frowned slightly and rearranged the placement of a silver spoon, aligning it precisely with the others beside the pink-and-white china plate.

At the sound of voices and laughter, she turned to see a

group of her young houseguests coming up from the tennis courts at the lower end of the lawn. They were chattering and swinging their rackets as they approached. She couldn't help smiling. How attractive they looked in the new requisite tennis costumes—the young women, in their starched white cotton blouses and hopsacking skirts; the young men, in white flannel trousers and shirts.

Noting that none of the girls wore hats, it was all Garnet could do to hold her tongue. Her first thought was to remind them of the damage the sun could do their tender young complexions. In *her* day, a girl *never* went without the protection of a bonnet and parasol. Still, no one had to remind Garnet that times had changed, so she closed her mouth and kept her good advice to herself.

Her eyes focused on her daughter who, with Jeff, had lagged a little behind the rest. What on earth could those two be talking about so intently? she wondered with a nagging uneasiness.

Jeff looked more and more like his father, Malcolm, with each passing year. He had the same smile, the same eyes, the same devastating Montrose charm. Garnet felt a quick, sharp fear for her daughter. From her own heartbreak, she knew that charm often masked a weakness of character and she hoped that Faith was not being taken in by Jeff's inherited good looks.

Her nebulous thought was diverted by the arrival of the maids, supervised by Hadley, bearing large trays laden with tea fare, and she set about to direct the placement.

"Good game?" Garnet asked as the young players reached the shadow of the trees.

With an admiring look at Faith, Neil replied, "Your daughter's much too good. I'd rather have her as a partner than an opponent any day!"

"It's my new racket," explained Faith with a self-deprecating laugh as she and Jeff joined the others around the tea table.

"What a smashing tea, Mrs. Devlin. I'm famished!" said Roy Hastings, a freckled redhead, eyeing a dainty watercress sandwich.

"Well, I thought perhaps you might have worked up an appetite by now," laughed Garnet. "Come, do help yourself."

"Don't tell him that, Mrs. Devlin," protested Tom Pullham in mock alarm. "He won't leave anything for the rest of us!"

"I'll watch him, don't worry—he won't take more than his share, I'll see to that, Mrs. Devlin," offered one of the pretty girls.

Garnet smiled happily. Surrounded by the lively company of the younger set, being flattered by the young men and admired by the young women, she was in her element. She so relished the teasing and gaiety. If only Faith enjoyed it more—

The young people were soon filling their plates with the tiny triangles spread with cucumber, tomato, and salmon paste, and quenching their thirst with large quantities of iced tea served from a frosted silver pitcher. In the center of the table on a glass pedestal stood a lemon sponge cake ready to be sliced. The cake, dusted with powdered sugar, was surrounded with luscious whole strawberries.

At that moment Garnet glanced at her daughter, just in time to see Faith pop a ripe red strawberry into Jeff's accommodating open mouth, and she watched as they both dissolved into laughter. At the intimacy of the little gesture, Neil Blanding's nice gray eyes clouded in dismay. He watched as Faith and Jeff took their plates and went a little apart from the others.

Unaware that they were being observed, Faith settled into a

chair with her plate of sandwiches while Jeff lowered himself onto the springy grass carpet alongside her. In low voices they continued whatever they had been discussing on their way up from the tennis courts.

She must have a word with her daughter before tonight, Garnet decided. Perhaps it would even be wise to rearrange the seating at dinner.

Garnet felt a flicker of irritation. Didn't Faith realize that she was as much a hostess of this house party as her mother was? She should be behaving as one, not devoting herself exclusively to one guest! The young people had been invited for *her* benefit, particularly Neil Blanding and Lady Allison, whose importance to her future should not be overlooked. She would *certainly* have to remind Faith of her duties.

The talk around the tea table was mostly joking confrontation about the informal tournament they were conducting, and challenges for new games were issued and accepted. Garnet, keeping an eye on Faith and Jeff, was only half-listening. What *could* those two be up to?

When Hadley appeared, signaling a message, Garnet excused herself and quietly left the group to see what it was. The butler handed her a note that had just come, explaining the late arrival of some dinner guests. By the time Garnet returned to the congenial company at the tea table, she was annoyed to see that Jeff and Faith had taken off. Frowning, she saw the two white-clad figures walking down the winding path to the lake at the base of the Birchfields property.

*   *   *

"It's hard to explain exactly what happened, Faith," Jeff said, gesturing as they walked along the path checkered by the sunlight filtering through the trees overhead. "It was just a kind of inner *knowing* that this is what I should do. It may

24

sound strange, but it was as if I heard a voice saying, 'Painting will be both your life's work and your joy!'" Here Jeff turned abruptly and demanded, "You think I've lost my mind, don't you?"

"No, Jeff! Of course I don't!" Faith protested.

"Well, I'm sure my stepfather will, though I don't know for certain." Jeff shrugged his shoulders and continued walking. "But one thing, I *do* know—I'll never go back to Virginia. That is, if I ever *do* return, it won't be to Cameron Hall to raise horses. It will be to Avalon . . . you know, the house on the island where my mother and I lived before she married Rod. Mum deeded it to me before her marriage. Everything in it . . . well, anyway, the library and the part of the house she had transported from England . . . is mine. And my grandfather, Jedediah Dorman, my mother's father, left an estate worth a great deal of money in trust for me. I'll inherit when I turn twenty-one." Jeff paused again, slanting a searching look at Faith. "That birthday's in *August*."

"Yes, I know."

"Well, at twenty-one a person is considered an adult, you know, ready to manage his own affairs, to do what he wants—" He paused. "I may be jumping the gun a bit—but I know *this* is what I want to do—what I *must* do."

"But you won't be able to until August—" Faith began, then added doubtfully— "will you?"

"Can you keep a secret, Faith? I mean, *absolutely?*"

"Of course I can, Jeff."

"I'm planning to take the check Mum sent me for my ship's ticket to Virginia this summer and use it to go to Europe!"

"Oh, Jeff!" gasped Faith.

"After I arrive, I'll write them a full explanation. . . . It's not as if I'd be *stealing* the money or anything. The check is made out to me. I'm just going to spend it on a ticket to somewhere else." He hesitated, waiting for her reaction. Then, flinging out his hands dramatically, he burst out, "I've got to see some of the great paintings in the museums and galleries of France, Italy, Spain! See them for *myself*, not just look at reproductions in art books. You understand, don't you, Faith? If I'm going to be an artist, I must go where the masters painted, where they lived and worked. I have to find out what inspired the pre-Raphaelite painters here in England."

"P—pre-Raphaelite painters?" Faith faltered, hating to display her ignorance but needing to know what was driving Jeff.

"You see, in London recently, I saw an exhibit of some of the most remarkable paintings. They spoke to something deep inside me. It was almost—" Jeff's expression had taken on a faraway quality, and Faith held her breath, waiting for him to go on— "almost as if I'd painted them myself . . . that is, if I were an artist. These painters formed themselves into a—a sort of brotherhood, with the highest ideals for themselves and their work. Painting was really more than a profession. It was a way of life for them . . . a blend of poetry, legend, religion, art. They chose great themes for their paintings from the Bible, from the epic stories of the past, like King Arthur and the Knights of the Round Table—"

Jeff's eyes were sparkling, and he was speaking rapidly in a voice charged with emotion. In spite of her misgivings, Faith felt herself swept up by his enthusiasm.

"You see, Faith, their beliefs blend with my own feelings about the way life ought to be—a devotion to what is fine, beautiful, pure. But first, of course, I have to learn to paint!" Jeff ran his hand through his thick, dark hair. "I *know* I can. I enjoyed rendering in my architectural studies but hated the mathematics, the geometry—all the dull drudgery involved in eventually creating something beautiful. I began to realize that it wasn't what I want to do. Faith, I've been miserable the last few months at Oxford. I *have* to get away and find out who I really am—do what I'm meant to do."

"But what will your mother say, and Uncle Rod?" Faith's voice was faint. The recklessness of Jeff's plan frightened her.

"They'll just have to accept it, that's all," Jeff said flatly, although there was a troubled look in his eyes. "And they won't know until I'm gone—then it will be too late for them to do anything about it!"

"But how will you live? Will you have enough money?"

"Enough. I'll live cheaply until August. You can, in Europe, you know, if you travel light. I intend to walk as much as possible, avoid passenger trains. I'll certainly *not* travel first class, in any event." He laughed. "I'll live simply, eat simply—bread, cheese, fruit—it shouldn't be hard, not hard at all for someone like me, Faith." Jeff smiled a disarming smile. "You knew, didn't you, that my grandmother was a Spanish gypsy? Wanderlust is probably in my blood."

He let out a whoop and spun around, throwing up his arms ecstatically. "Oh, Faith, I can't tell you how free I feel now that I've made this decision!"

In contrast, she felt a heaviness lodged in her own chest. "How long will you be away?" she ventured meekly.

"I don't know. I'll want to come back to England, of course, to take some courses at the Royal Academy of Art to get my basics. To be accepted as an artist here, that kind of background is required. But there's time enough for that. First, I've got to see with my own eyes the kind of paintings I want to do myself—absorb the genius of the past, walk the same streets, breathe the same air as those artists who created the great masterpieces that are my inspiration—though I'll want to interpret them in my own way, of course."

He took Faith by the shoulders and looked deeply into her eyes. "Trust me, Faith. Believe in me, wish me luck, and give me your blessing!"

Jeff's smile transformed his face and lighted his eyes with a burning intensity that caused Faith to hold her breath. Surely Jeff was inspired, surely this was what he was supposed to do. If she could only be sure, she could reconcile herself to his going away for . . . who knew how long?

chapter
3

ON MONDAY morning after breakfast, all the houseguests, including Jeff, gathered in the front hall before departing to go their separate ways. It was the moment Faith had dreaded all weekend. She would have to pretend that it was just like any other parting after a house party. Not even Jeff knew that, at least for her, it was vastly different. His secret weighed heavily upon her.

Faith walked out onto the terrace. The servants were bustling back and forth, carrying out the luggage and securing it at the back of the Devlins' carriage that would carry them all to the train station in the village. Then she took her place beside her parents to receive the thanks expressed by grateful guests and to hear the promise of future plans to meet again soon at some party or other to which they were all invited. It devastated Faith to realize that Jeff would not be present at any of these. Worse, she didn't have the slightest idea as to when she would see him again.

The added pressure of his hand on hers when he stood before her at last and the look in his eyes told her he trusted her. Then he bent down to brush her cheek with his lips and to whisper that he would be writing to let her know where he was and that she must write back.

But there had never been time for Faith to say what was in her heart to say to Jeff, all the things she longed to tell him. They had had less time alone than usual this weekend. Was it her imagination, Faith wondered, or had her mother seemed particularly watchful? Just about the time she and Jeff had launched into a serious topic, here had come Garnet, almost appearing to invent excuses for Faith to be with Neil Blanding, or to show Mrs. Canning the rose garden, or to fill in as a fourth at bridge.

Somehow Faith had managed to survive it all—up until the last dreadful moments when she realized that Jeff was actually leaving. With anguished eyes she watched him go down the terrace steps, swing his long, lean frame into the carriage with a final, jaunty wave of his hand. Frantically, she waved back. The horses started to move and the carriage jolted forward down the drive. Then he was gone.

Faith's arms dropped to her sides. She turned away and walked back into the house, her throat aching with the tears she had forced back. Before she could betray her feelings, she ran upstairs and down the corridor until she reached her room. There she flung herself face downward on the bed and gave way to the storm that had been gathering within her all weekend.

She never knew how long she lay there sobbing. When at last she finally stopped, she sat up, breathless. All the tears in the world would not ease the pain she was feeling. If this was the way a heart feels when it is broken, hers surely was.

Sometime, somewhere, Faith had read a beautiful poem, perhaps translated from the Russian. It said in part, that anyone who loves must suffer, for "who has found a rose without a thorn?"

Faith knew that she loved Jeff, but *he* did not know it. And maybe he would never know. So much could happen before they saw each other again.

He was gone, and the awful emptiness of her world without the hope of seeing him, overwhelmed her.

*   *   *

Back in Oxford, Jeff made quick work of tying up loose ends and completing plans for his departure to France. Despite the caution advised by his tutors and instructors and the half-envious, half-satirical comments of his friends, he was determined. Spurred on by his vision of a quest that would bring him both spiritual enlightenment and a lifelong purpose, a kind of religious fervor had seized him. Nothing could stop him now. He would not rest until he had taken up the original goals of the artists whose work he admired so much.

On the day he was to leave, Jeff was clearing out his rooms, stacking the belongings he was leaving in a corner to be carted away after he left. One of his best friends, Kevin Branch, lounged on Jeff's stripped bed, watching as he finished packing.

"Could you use another one of these?" Jeff asked jokingly, holding out his black academic gown worn by Oxford University undergraduates. "I have no further use for it. I'm off to a life of adventure and excitement."

"It wouldn't take much for me to chuck it all and come along with you, old man," Kevin remarked. "But my pater would cut me off without a shilling if I dared such a thing!"

Jeff shook his head. "Sometimes you have to take that kind of risk. I don't know what the repercussions of my decision are going to be for me. But I have to find out for myself if what I believe I should do is the right thing. You can't spend your whole life doing what other people *think* you should do."

31

"It's different for you." Kevin seemed slightly defensive. "You're coming into some money of your own on your birthday, right?"

"It's not all that much—just a house on an island in Virginia and a trust fund that will give me a yearly dividend. I don't even know what it will amount to, actually."

"Yes, but from what you've told me, the library in that house contains some first editions. You could sell those and live like a king for some time on what they'd bring."

"I'm not planning to sell anything. Someday I plan to live there and paint. Anyhow, that's my thinking now."

Kevin got up and stretched leisurely. "Well, I wish you the best of luck, old chap," he said with a last lingering look at Jeff's bulging knapsack. "I can't help feeling a tad jealous of your freedom. You'll have some grand experiences, no doubt—" He paused, still eying Jeff's stack of belongings ready to be stuffed into the canvas bag. "France, first, eh? Then Spain?"

"Yes, Spain. I went there with my mother as a boy, but I don't remember too much about it—except that it was always sunny and warm, and I played with some other children—" Jeff's voice trailed off nostalgically. "I've Spanish blood myself, you see, and I feel . . . well, I don't know what I feel exactly . . . only that I can't wait to reach Seville, especially."

Kevin thrust out his hand and Jeff clasped it in a firm grip. The two young men looked at each other for a moment before his classmate clapped Jeff on the shoulder and started out of the room. At the door he turned and gave a smart salute.

"Goodbye, good luck, and God bless," he said with some embarrassment, then he was gone.

Jeff stood for a few minutes staring at the closed door, then began cramming the rest of his things into his knapsack. He straightened up and surveyed the room with a last sweeping look to see if he was forgetting anything. He checked the bookcase, its shelves empty now. Then his glance fell on the table by the bed.

There he saw a well-worn copy of Tennyson's *Idylls of the King*. He went over, picked it up, and flipped it open to the flyleaf. The inscription, written in faded ink, read: "To my dear son, Malcolm—a real knight in shining armor. From his loving mother, Sara Leighton Montrose." The father he had never known, the grandmother he had met only once.

His mother had given him the book some years earlier, telling him it had been his father's favorite. Strange, how the stories of the knights of King Arthur had always held a fascination for him, too. Even his house in Virginia— Avalon—had been named for the island where legend had it that the wounded King Arthur was taken after his last battle with the evil Mordred.

Jeff had cut his teeth on the traditions of valor, truth, faith, courage, and honor espoused by Arthur and his knights. And why shouldn't men live their lives governed by these ideals? It was how he intended to live his.

Suddenly it all fell into place. The dream he so recently had discovered in himself seemed as much a sacred quest to him as those the legendary young men had pursued to attain their knighthood. Maybe it also explained why he had fallen under the spell of the painters who had captured forever on canvas the most noble themes known to man.

He took the book and stuffed it into his knapsack, fastened the buckles on the straps, slung it over his shoulders, and with a final look around the room he had occupied at Oxford for the last year and a half, he went out the door, letting it slam shut behind him.

chapter

4

FAITH COUNTED off the next few weeks of summer, trying to imagine where Jeff might be. Surreptitiously she checked the post when it arrived each morning to see if there might be some word from him. All in vain. Of course, she knew that he did not want to put her in the hazardous position of knowing what he intended to do until after his letter had reached his parents in Virginia. All the same, she ached with worry and missed him more than she had thought possible.

Outwardly she went through the motions required of her as a soon-to-be debutante—the dressmaker fittings, the luncheons, the parties, the invitations that must be acknowledged and accepted, the calls she must make with her mother. But she was totally preoccupied.

Puzzled, Garnet often quizzed Faith as to why she turned down so many of the social invitations that flooded Birchfields' post for her. But Faith didn't confide in her mother the real reason that she was so little interested.

On the rare evenings when no engagement required her attendance, Faith took long twilight walks down the winding garden paths or the woodland trail that led to the lake. She had often strolled these same paths with Jeff and should have been consoled. But a kind of melancholy had overshadowed her since his departure, one she could not shake, no matter what she did.

Then one evening when she returned from her solitary walk, Garnet was standing at the drawing room door. Something in her mother's expression sent a chill through Faith.

"Come in here, please, dear. Your father and I want to talk to you." Garnet's tone was brittle.

She followed her mother into the room. Garnet walked over to her desk, picked up an envelope, and handed it to her. "What do you know about this?"

Faith took the letter, noting the Virginia, USA postmark. Then, with widened eyes, she looked at her mother.

"Go on, read it. It's from Jeff's mother, Blythe Cameron."

Even before she withdrew the sheets of thin paper from the envelope and began to read, Faith's heart was beating hard. The words on the pages seemed to run together, blurring as her eyes moved back and forth across the lines, absorbing all the bewilderment, shock, and hurt expressed by Jeff's mother. Faith sympathized with the woman. But she also understood now why Jeff had chosen to follow his own dream. If he had not, he might forever be a prisoner of Blythe Cameron's possessive love.

When Faith finally looked up from the letter she held in both hands, her mother's eyes seared her.

"Did you know what Jeff was planning to do?" Garnet demanded.

"Yes. He told me that last weekend he was down here."

"Don't you think it was your responsibility, your *duty* to tell us?" Garnet did not try to conceal her indignation.

"No, Mama. It was Jeff's decision."

"Decision? A mere boy making such a decision?"

"Jeff isn't a boy, Mama. He's nearly twenty-one."

"Then he shouldn't *behave* like a boy!" Garnet retorted, snatching the letter. "To take money his parents sent him to go home to Virginia, then take off for who knows where? Is that the act of a responsible twenty-one-year-old *man?*"

Faith had no answer. She glanced at her father sitting silently in his comfortable leather chair. As yet, he had said nothing.

Garnet began to pace back and forth, stopping every once in a while to give the short train of her dress a little kick, tapping her fingers impatiently on the letter she still held.

"His mother seems to think it's somehow *our* fault," she declared. "I suppose she's written the Ainsleys as well. But how on earth could we have prevented something we knew nothing about?" She whirled around and speared Faith with another reproachful look. "I do think that you should have shown more judgment, Faith. If Jeff confided in you, you should have—"

"That's just it, Mama. Jeff *did* confide in me, and I wouldn't betray that trust. Besides, I believe in what he's doing. I think he could be a great artist."

Garnet gave a small, scoffing sound. "Artist, indeed! He's never shown any particular talent in art before, that I know of."

"He *was* studying architecture at Oxford, wasn't he, my dear?" Jeremy put in mildly.

"But that's entirely different." Garnet turned to address her husband. "Architecture's a respectable profession—"

"But one would have to have an artistic bent, an understanding of structure, knowledge of design, an appreciation of beauty to become an architect, I would think," Jeremy continued. "The young man probably had an inherent talent that he has just discovered in himself."

Garnet slapped the envelope into the upturned palm of her hand and gave a frustrated sigh.

"Well, that has nothing to do with this present problem, Jeremy. What am I to tell Blythe and Rod? That Jeff has been under my roof a half-dozen times since Christmas, and I knew nothing about his plans? It sounds incredible."

"Perhaps, but true. All you can do is write that this is as much a surprise to us as to them—" he suggested.

"Except to our daughter!" Garnet glared at Faith.

Faith lowered her eyes but did not reply.

"Well, blood will tell, as they say," Garnet said finally. "Jeff has a wild, reckless streak in him. His mother's mother was a gypsy dancer, you know!"

Faith bit her lip, suppressing the urge to rush to Jeff's defense. In her mind, his Spanish blood only gave him an even more dashing, romantic aura. But this she would never reveal. Not to anyone. Least of all, to her mother.

chapter
5
Summer 1893

STANDING at her bedroom window, Faith looked down into Belvedere Square, the wooded park facing the Devlins' impressive London town house. Not a leaf was stirring on this hot August morning, a sure sign that it would get even hotter. In spite of the heat, dreading the day ahead, she shivered involuntarily.

Why had she ever agreed to this madness? She had never wanted to be presented at Court. That was her mother's dream, the crowning glory of the debutante year. After this, maybe, just maybe, she would be able to lead her own life.

Faith picked up the teacup Annie had brought up to her earlier and took a sip just as a brisk rapping sounded at the door.

"Good morning, my darling. Well, the big day at last!" Garnet exclaimed as she rustled in, looking incredibly young and lovely in a lacy peignoir, ruffles fluttering and ribbons flying as she flitted happily about the room. Pausing to admire Faith's presentation gown hanging from the folding screen by the armoire, she fingered the filmy folds of the chiffon overskirt.

"Oh, it *is* exquisite," she sighed. "You'll be the outstanding debutante there!"

For the first time, she focused her full attention on Faith. "You're looking a little pale, dear. Are you feeling quite all right?" Then she swept across the room and touched her daughter's cheek and forehead with a cool hand. "Probably just the excitement. It's not *every* day that a Virginian meets the Queen of England! Now, come. You'll have to start dressing soon to be ready on time. Lydia said she would be sending the carriage at quarter of twelve."

"That seems terribly early, doesn't it, Mother? I mean— when the presentations don't begin until three?" began Faith.

"Perhaps, but evidently that's how it's done. Lydia says the carriages line up outside the palace for blocks, waiting their turn. Each is given a place and—well, *she* ought to know!" Garnet frowned slightly. "I wish it were possible for me to go, too. But only one sponsor is allowed with each presentee."

Faith knew that it bothered her mother terribly that she would not be able to see her only daughter's presentation to Queen Victoria.

"Well, that can't be helped," said Garnet practically. "Now, I'll be running along. When you're dressed, I'll come back to see you in all your glory." She patted Faith's cheek and sailed out the door, calling over her shoulder, "I'll send Annie up to help you."

Annie Pratt, the butler's niece, had been trained by Garnet's maid and brought along from Birchfields to attend to Faith's needs during her London season. But the idea of being dressed and combed by a girl nearly her own age still seemed extravagant and silly. In spite of both mothers' instructions, though, the two young women had become friends.

Annie's mum had cautioned her to "remember your place," and Garnet had urged Faith against confiding in a servant.

39

"No matter how loyal they may seem, they like to gossip 'downstairs'," Garnet had warned.

As it turned out, both young women had ignored their mothers' advice. Annie was Faith's "safety valve" for, if ever there was one, Faith was a reluctant debutante. It was no secret between the two of them that had it not been for her mother's pride and satisfaction, she would have much preferred to decline the honor of being presented at Court.

Following a discreet tap, a quiet voice came at the door. "It's Annie, miss." Then the bedroom door opened slightly, admitting a small, thin girl in a black dress and ruffled white cap and apron.

"Your mother wanted me to tell you it's time, miss."

"Is it?" Faith asked indifferently. "Yes, I guess it is, Annie." Putting down her empty cup, she looked at her maid with resignation. "Then let's get it over with."

With no further discussion, they set about the necessary and involved preparation. First, Faith's hair must be arranged. Her thick, naturally curly mane was the bane of her existence, since it stubbornly defied any effort at styling. But Faith had gradually begun to consider it a blessing. At least she did not have to try to sleep in paper curlers nor withstand the long process of crimping irons she had heard the other debs complaining about. By now, however, Annie had become quite expert in doing it up in record time, and had helped her mistress achieve a simple but becoming hairstyle.

That chore out of the way, Annie helped Faith off with her negligee. She suppressed a groan as Annie began lacing her into her whalebone corset to make her slim waist appear even tinier. Over this went a lace-trimmed camisole followed by two petticoats—one cotton, one taffeta.

"Now, miss, your gown," said Annie as she brought down the creation of pale pink satin from its hanger. Standing behind Faith, she helped her step into the underskirt and fastened the band at the back. The bodice was separate, put on like a jacket, with Annie breathing hard from the task of hooking a dozen or more tiny concealed hooks and eyes. The satin underdress in place, the chiffon overskirt was then dropped over her head and arranged.

After Faith was buttoned and snapped, she tried to take a deep breath but found it impossible. The bodice already felt miserably tight and hot. She gritted her teeth in helpless frustration. How ridiculous on this humid summer day to be donning a ball gown! And how could she endure this torture trap for four hours or more?

Regarding herself bleakly in the full-length mirror, she could not resist asking, "What am I doing?"

Before she could attempt an answer, her mother was back. "Oh, my dear, you're a vision! I've never seen you look so elegant! A real princess, isn't she, Annie?" Garnet circled Faith, observing her from every angle.

"Now, Annie, let's put on her headpiece," Garnet directed the maid. "The Ainsleys' coach will be here any minute."

The maid handed her the narrow band of pearls, and Garnet placed it carefully on Faith's head, securing it with pearl-headed pins before attaching the requisite three white plumes.

"There now, perfect!" she said, stepping back and nodding in approval.

The last item of the specified attire for a Court presentation was the satin train, held with small loops to the shoulders of Faith's gown. It took both Garnet and Annie to fasten it and carry it as Faith made her way stiffly down the stairway and out to the Ainsleys' carriage, waiting just outside the front door. Perhaps, if she thought of happier things—of Jeff, for example—the hours would pass more pleasantly.

*   *   *

The tedious wait in the line of carriages lasted two hours but seemed an eternity to Faith. Sitting erect so as not to wrinkle her gown and the cape with its shirred chiffon lining, Faith's neck began to ache. She put up her hand to massage the taut muscles and in doing so, shifted the elaborate headdress, then guiltily straightened it.

Why in the world had she allowed herself to be a party to this senseless charade? Who cared whether she was presented to the Queen? She knew the answer, of course. Her mother cared. To Garnet, a Court presentation represented the pinnacle of social achievement.

Faith glanced at the other occupants of the stifling carriage. Mrs. Ainsley was managing to look cool and composed in a lovely green French voile dress, her necklace and earrings of emeralds and pearls becoming accents to her English good looks.

Because Lydia Ainsley was Jeff's godmother, Faith had been particularly eager to know her better. During the debutante year, when Lydia had been her chaperone for all the social events to which they were invited, Faith had discovered that the woman's warmth was real—her kindness, genuine. But it was her radiant serenity, so different from her own mother's volatile personality, that had fascinated Faith, and she longed to know the secret.

She was pleased when, one afternoon while returning from an afternoon of calls, Lydia had squeezed Faith's hand impulsively and begun speaking quietly.

"I feel so lucky to be a part of all this with you and Allison, dear. For years Edward and I prayed for children of our own and could not understand why God didn't answer our prayers. Now I know He has. You see, Faith, I found a verse

42

in the Psalms that was God's own precious promise to me: "He maketh the barren woman . . . to be a joyful mother of children." And that's exactly what He did when he gave me you and Allison as if you were truly my daughters. And, of course, my darling Jeff, who has meant as much to me as any son born to me ever could."

Remembering that declaration of love, Faith saw the evidence again in the tender gaze Lydia now turned on her niece, Lady Allison, who was radiant with excitement and anticipation.

Dismally Faith wondered why *she* couldn't be like Allison and the other young women she had met during this year. Why did she have to feel so different, so rebellious, so indifferent to the things the others found enjoyable?

The main reason, perhaps, was that she wasn't looking for a husband. Most of the debutantes, certainly their mamas, were willing to put up with the discomfort and tedium of events such as this in the interest of attracting suitable marriage prospects. It was hoped that this would lead to a fashionable wedding and a prestigious place in society. None of which Faith wanted.

What do *I want?* she asked herself. *Jeff,* came the answer. *Yes, I want Jeff and the kind of life I would have with him—a life of beauty, high ideals, romantic adventure—Oh, Jeff, where are you?*

Faith looked out the carriage window at the crowds milling along the sidewalks. They stared back, gawking at the mannequin-like creatures inside, arrayed like costume dolls on display.

Faith closed her eyes for a moment to shut them out, thinking of the dark green wooded acres of Birchfields. She could be riding Bounty right now, the cool breeze off the lake blowing on her face, sending her hair out in streamers behind her.

Just then the carriage jerked forward, wobbling slightly, and Mrs. Ainsley smiled at her reassuringly. "Ah, we're moving on, at last. I don't think it will be too much longer now, girls."

Faith felt herself stiffen, reminding herself that once this was over, there would only be one more hurdle—the reception her parents were giving tonight in her honor. *Actually,* Faith thought with a stab of resentment, *it is more* Mother's *party to celebrate my successful launch into society.* Then the season was almost over. Except for her ball to be held at Birchfields at the end of the summer. If Jeff could only be there, not wandering all over Europe—

Her longing thoughts were brought to an end as the carriage came to a shaky stop.

"Here we are, girls!" announced Mrs. Ainsley. "Are you ready to meet the Queen?"

*　　*　　*

Late that night, too stimulated for sleep, Faith curled up in bed to write a letter to Jeff. She would mail it to the most recent address he had scribbled on a postcard—General Delivery, Post Office, Florence, Italy.

Before starting the letter, she had taken out the small packet of battered picture postcards from Paris, Rome, and Verona that had arrived after long intervals from Jeff. On most of them he had scrawled only a few enigmatic remarks. But she had read them over and over, studying the pictures of the Coliseum, St. Peter's, the Tuileries Gardens, until she knew every word, every line by heart. Doggedly she had continued to write, never sure that he received her letters, since he never commented on anything she said. She poured out her heart to

Jeff, telling him all the details of her summer, withholding only the secret of her love for him.

Oh, Jeff, you could not imagine the crush! After we got out of the carriage, we were herded like sheep into a small room in the palace, where we had to wait again. It was hot and airless, and two of the girls fainted and had to be carried away. I don't know whether they missed their presentation time or what. If so, there are several mamas who went to bed with migraines tonight, you can be sure!

When it finally came my turn, I was so dulled from boredom that I didn't hear my name called. Someone literally had to push me forward! Somehow I managed to meet the Queen without tripping over my feet or getting tangled in my train.

I made my curtsy and took a quick look at Her Majesty, who is a small, fat old lady, dressed in black, with a rather sullen expression and heavy-lidded eyes. I wonder if she was even aware of all the trouble we had all gone through to be presented to her—or if she cared?

Do you intend to come back soon? I wish I knew your plans. By fall I should be free of all this "debutante" rubbish, and if you come down to Birchfields, we'll go riding and have some good times just like we used to!

Faith paused, her pen poised over the paper. Would that ever really happen again? Or would Jeff have changed so much that they would never be able to recapture their old camaraderie? Had art consumed him so that he would be lost to her forever even after he returned?

And how should she sign the letter? "All my love," which would be truthful, or the more discreet, "As ever?" She sighed. The latter was just as true, since she loved Jeff as she always had, no matter how she put it.

chapter

6

London, England
Spring 1894

FAITH WAS ecstatic when she received Jeff's note, inviting her
to accompany him to the Opening Day of the annual exhibit
at the Royal Academy of Art on the first Monday in May.

She had seen very little of Jeff since his return from his
"vagabond year" in Europe. He had come back lean and
tanned, with a sketchbook full of people he had met and
places he had been, and an undiminished determination to
become an artist. At first he had come down to Birchfields
often, regaling Faith with stories of his adventures and
enthusiastic descriptions of the museums and works of art he
had seen.

Anxious to share what was most important to him, to learn
about the pre-Raphaelite painters and other artists Jeff
admired, Faith had tried to educate herself about art and
painting so that she could not only listen but speak intelli-
gently about them. As it turned out, however, there was little
opportunity to do so.

After he had enrolled in the Royal Academy of Art, taking

as many classes as he was allowed, Jeff's world began to revolve around his studies and the instructors and fellow students at the Academy. His visits to the country became more infrequent, and when he found lodgings with an artist friend that boasted a small studio where they could paint, the Devlins saw even less of Jeff.

Until his invitation, Faith did not know when she could expect to see Jeff again. He had spent Christmas in London with the Ainsleys and, although he had promised to come down for the Devlins' annual New Year's Ball at Birchfields, he had contracted a heavy cold and was unable to make it even then.

With so much time having elapsed, Faith was especially eager to look her best for the Opening Day. What should she wear? Jeff's note had been casual, mentioning only that they would go somewhere afterward for tea. That could be anywhere! When she was with Jeff, Faith was aware of feminine heads turning to observe his dark, Byronic good looks. She would just have to do something to be sure that *he* concentrated on *her*.

At last she decided on an ensemble newly acquired, one that Jeff had never seen—a peacock-blue light wool walking suit with wide darker blue satin revers on the fitted jacket. With it she would wear a daring little tilted hat with a dotted blue veil and gloves to match.

But the fact that Faith had taken such pains with her appearance was apparently lost on Jeff, who was in such a hurry to get to the exhibit that when he met her at the train, he rushed her into a waiting taxi with scarcely more than a greeting. Perhaps later, over tea, he would mention her new outfit, she told herself. He usually noticed such things.

On the way, Jeff rattled off the names of some of the artists whose paintings had been accepted by the Academy. Some

47

choices he applauded, others he disagreed with, saying that some really fine artists whose paintings deserved to be hung, had been rejected.

Within a block of the Royal Academy there was a jam of carriages. The horses, prancing skittishly, made it difficult for drivers to maintain their places in line so that their occupants could be safely delivered.

"Opening Day is always a crush!" declared Jeff, peering anxiously out the coach window. "Maybe we should get out here and walk the rest of the way."

Faith winced, remembering her new high-heeled boots that had not been designed for walking and especially not for keeping up with Jeff's long-legged stride. To distract him from this suggestion, Faith quickly asked a question.

"Will all the exhibitors be there today?"

"Oh, you couldn't keep them away!" replied Jeff. "The exhibit is open to the public today, so exhibitors can mill around and not be too obvious as they strain their ears for comments from the critics and art reporters who will be here in full force—" He smiled wryly. "And naturally, if they're recognized, to accept compliments on their work. Oh, Faith, what I wouldn't give to be one of them! But I will be one day. You'll see." His jaw tightened and Faith could feel his intensity.

"Yes, Jeff, I'm sure you will," she said loyally.

"Imagine, what it must be like—" he murmured, and Faith saw his hands ball into fists, one of which he thrummed tensely on his knee. Then he turned to look at her, eyes shining. "The Prince of Wales and the Queen, if she's well enough, come on the Thursday before Opening Day to view the selected paintings in private. Friday is Private View, by invitation only. I've heard that some consider this to be the beginning of the social season. Tom and I came and stood along the curb to see the arrivals. Quite spectacular. Splendid carriages pulling up in front. The ladies, dressed 'to the nines'; the gentlemen, in morning coats and top hats. Some of the viewers were minor royalty, members of Parliament and their ladies." Jeff gave a little laugh. "I wonder how many *real* art lovers there were among them. I suspect most of them simply came to see and be seen."

When their taxi finally pushed up the line, a good half-block from the Academy, Jeff opened the door impatiently, paid the fare, and reached in to help Faith out.

Inside, the artists who had been successful in having their work hung were present in hordes. Art critics and society reporters, tell-tale notebooks in hand, scurried about, seeking interviews from the more famous. Jeff recognized some not-so-well-known painters, too, and mumbled their names to Faith as they jockeyed for attention, hoping to be noticed and to receive favorable comments or reviews.

In the press of people, Faith had a hard time keeping up with Jeff as he elbowed his way through. She could barely see the paintings, much less appreciate or enjoy them. Hat askew, face flushed, and tottering in her untried new boots, Faith was grateful when Jeff had had enough.

"Let's go, this is a madhouse!" he said. "We'll have to come back later in the week when we can really see something." Taking her hand and turning a broad shoulder to the crowd, he pushed back through the incoming crush blocking the door through which they had come earlier.

Outside, Faith straightened the brim of her hat and adjusted her veil while Jeff ran a short distance to hail a taxi. Almost before she could catch her breath, they were drawing up in front of a fine hotel, and the taxi door was being opened by a uniformed doorman.

"My, are you sure *this* is the place?" Faith whispered as they entered the grand lobby of Claridge's.

"After putting you through all that, I think you deserve a posh tea," he replied confidently and guided her toward the dining room, where a dignified maitre d'hotel bowed in greeting and a waiter escorted them to a corner table.

After being seated, a worried little pucker appeared between her dark brows. Leaning toward him, Faith asked Jeff in a low tone, "Are you positive you can afford this?"

Jeff laughed the rich, full laugh that Faith loved.

"Of course, my dear old worrywart," he assured her. "Didn't you know I've come into my inheritance? First of the month, regular as Big Ben, my cheque from the trust fund arrives. I've not paid my school fees or rent as yet, so order away—the sky is the veritable limit—strawberry trifle, sponge cake, chocolate éclairs—whatever your little heart desires!"

"Well, in that case," declared Faith, entering into the game, "tell the waiter to bring the entire dessert trolley!"

Within a few minutes the first awkwardness of the long months apart disappeared, and Faith and Jeff were back on their old terms, teasing and bantering with one another. She could see that Jeff was still stimulated from the exhibit, and although she would much rather have turned the conversation to more personal things, he was too wound up to speak of anything else.

"I didn't see much today. At least, nothing I would call avant-garde," he commented as he offered Faith the plate of buttered scones, then helped himself. "That's why I admire the pre-Raphaelite artists so much. *They* tried to break through the stuffiness."

"What do you mean? I don't quite understand." Faith was genuinely interested.

"Well, before they—the pre-Raphaelites—came on the scene, there were rigid rules to which paintings and artists had to adhere, such as the subjects the Royal Academy would consider suitable for hanging in the annual exhibit," Jeff explained. "More tea?"

Faith held out her cup.

"Even the *position* a painting was hung was restricted. I mean, it was all so political, you see. Placement of one's painting at the exhibit depended on an artist's rank and rating in the judgment of the hanging committee."

"The hanging committee?"

"A handful of men whose vision was very limited," Jeff replied scornfully, reaching for the thick raspberry jam and piling it liberally on his scone.

"And what did the pre-Raphaelites do to change things?" Faith was leaning forward now, her tea growing cold in her cup.

"Rossetti, Millais, and Holman Hunt were trying to do something new, yet still based on medieval art. They wanted to use a broader palette, richer colors. What they wanted to do was to bring back the romantic idealism of the great Italian artists before Raphael. Actually, they hoped to restore what they felt had been lost. Get rid of all those murky landscapes—" Jeff made a grimace of disgust—"that awful drabness, the gloominess."

"But, Jeff—" Faith began somewhat tentatively, not sure enough of her ground to argue, yet wanting to show Jeff that she had done some research of her own on the subject. "Personally, I think some of *their* paintings are gloomy. Take Millais's painting of 'Ophelia.' What could be gloomier than a painting of a drowned girl with a ghastly pale face, floating on the surface of the water like—like seaweed!"

Jeff had to smile. "Well, yes, I have to admit that some of

51

the subjects were on the dark side." He signaled the waiter to bring them a fresh pot of tea, then continued. "But it's not just the richness and texture of their paintings that I'm talking about. It's their themes that inspire me. They used the great legends of King Arthur's knights. They used allegory, religion, poetry. That's what painting is all about to me— inspired and inspiring to painter and viewer alike."

"Oh, Jeff, yes! I do understand," Faith breathed, catching some of his enthusiasm.

"That's my goal, too, Faith. I want to paint the kind of paintings that will—how can I say it without sounding insufferably arrogant—" he paused, as if searching for the word.

"It doesn't sound arrogant at all," she said, then smiled. "A bit ambitious, perhaps?"

Jeff pushed his teacup aside, folded his arms, and leaned on them. "Ambition can be very close to arrogance. It's self-destructive, really. In a way, that's what led to Rossetti's downfall. He was the leader of the group, extremely talented and charismatic but too easily bored to put in the necessary apprenticeship and too impatient to learn perspective and composition. Some of his paintings show it. Figures out of proportion, perspective off—" Jeff dismissed this unsolicited critique with a wave of his hand and, smiling slightly, went on.

"Anyway, almost as a lark, Rossetti had offered to paint a huge mural in Oxford's Union Debating Hall, and filled the walls with elaborate scenes from the legends of Malory's *Morte d'Arthur*. He even volunteered several of his fellow artists to help, and they all went down to Oxford and had a high old time all one summer. The trouble was, none of them knew how to prepare plaster properly. As a result, the paint sank right into the surface, and now all that can be seen is a faint tracery of ghostly figures here and there."

"Oh, what a shame! What a waste of time and talent!" exclaimed Faith.

"Of course, that was the reason the original brotherhood fell apart. Each went his separate way, and some came to tragic ends, I'm afraid." Jeff sighed and shook his head. Then he lifted his chin, his eyes level with Faith's across the table.

"Their dream is now mine, Faith. I want to recreate a mural like Rossetti had in mind when he started—the legend of King Arthur, depicting the stories of his knights on panels in the style of the pre-Raphaelites, with all the drama and richness of texture and color they introduced. That's why I must learn everything I can at the Academy and from the Old Masters, and why I must paint and paint!"

Gripped by his intensity, Faith could hardly breathe.

"Oh, yes, Jeff, what a wonderful plan! I'm sure you will . . . you can!"

Slowly the fervent expression softened to a smile, the passionate light in his eyes became teasing again. "I believe if I said I was going to fly over the English Channel, you'd tell me I could do it, wouldn't you, Faith?"

Faith's cheeks grew warm and she tried to reply in the same light manner he had used. Though she knew in her heart that what he said was true, he did not suspect the reasons why.

"Well, I guess we'd best be going. I have a class tonight and you have a train to catch." Jeff rose, came around to pull out her chair and offer her his arm.

Settled inside the cab the doorman had hailed at the corner, Faith smiled at Jeff. "It was a perfect day. Thank you for asking me."

"I enjoyed it, too, Faith. But it will have to last us a while, I'm afraid. I'm leaving in two weeks for the south of France.

Provence. Tom and I are taking off to join a community of artists for a summer of painting. The light there is supposed to be incredible!"

The words that fell so lightly from Jeff's lips sank like weighted stones into Faith's heart. Jeff was going away again. Who knew when he would be back this time? Or how his experiences with a new group of kindred spirits would shape him? And what if, in that fabled country of lovers, he met someone who would capture his heart as Faith had not yet been able to do?

Part II

Invitation Extended
Invitation Received

A Family Reunion
Spring 1897

O call back yesterday, bid time return—
—Shakespeare, *Richard II*

chapter

7

Belvedere Square
London, England

WHEN FAITH came down to breakfast, her parents were already seated at the table. As she entered the dining room, her mother looked up.

"Good morning, darling." Garnet's bright smile faded as she watched her daughter bypass the chafing dish of eggs, the hot plate of bacon and sausages, the silver rack of toast on the well-laden sideboard and pour herself a cup of coffee. "Is that all you're having?"

"This is fine, Mummy. I'm really not hungry."

"That's no breakfast at all," Garnet declared reproachfully. "Certainly not when you're spending all day with Lydia Ainsley at that dreadful ... place."

Faith took a sip of coffee, bracing herself for one of her mother's tirades about her work at Hampton House. Garnet was vehemently opposed to her helping two days a week in the soup kitchen run by Lydia and a group of her like-minded friends.

Hoping to divert a prolonged argument before it began,

Faith glanced over at her father and caught the unspoken caution in the eyes regarding her over the top of his newspaper. She had to suppress a smile. Knowing him so well, she realized that he was hoping there wouldn't be one of the frequent clashes of will between the two strong-minded women in his family.

"Good morning, Papa."

"Good morning, my dear," replied Jeremy, trying to conceal his concern as he looked at his daughter. To his way of thinking, Faith was much too thin these days, her cheekbones sharp under the shadowed eyes. What was troubling her? Jeremy wished he knew. He had given her everything a daughter could possibly want—or at least, he had tried. Why then were her eyes often so sad, her smile so wistful? Could it be something she was hiding from them? Some unhappy love affair, some failed romance?

Jeremy knew that Garnet had hoped Faith would make a brilliant marriage following her debutante season. But that had not happened. Now Faith seemed less inclined than ever to participate in the social scene unless pressured into an obligatory attendance somewhere.

"So what do *you* think, Jeremy?"

The slightly annoyed tone in his wife's voice let him know he must have missed her question. As it turned out, it was Faith's enthusiastic response that gave him the gist of Garnet's proposal.

"A family reunion this summer at Birchfields?" Faith exclaimed. "Oh, I think that's a wonderful idea, Mummy. Do you suppose they will all come? Druscilla and the girls? Jonathan and Davida? And Uncle Rod and Jeff's mother, too?"

"Well, that's what I'm hoping. I'm writing them today so they'll have plenty of time to make their plans and book passage. They could probably all come on board the same ship. Wouldn't that be a lark? To have us all together again—wouldn't Mama have loved it?" Garnet paused for a moment, an expression of sadness clouding her face. "Actually, now that she's gone, I feel it's more important than ever for the rest of us to stay close. That is, as close as possible with everyone scattered to the ends of the earth! It's not like the good old days when Montclair and Cameron Hall were only a horseback ride away and we saw each other often."

"So when will they come?" Jeremy asked, now aware that the next major event on their social calendar would be a family house party.

"I've asked them to come at the end of May when we can be fairly sure the weather will be nice. Cool by Virginia standards, but pleasantly warm here. By then the gardens at Birchfields should be beautiful, and we can enjoy lots of outdoor activities—tennis, swimming, boating on the lake—And, of course, I'll plan some wonderful parties and supper dances for the young people." Garnet clapped her hands together girlishly. "Oh, it will be such fun!"

"And we can take them sightseeing as well," Faith suggested. "They'll want to see the Tower of London and Westminster Cathedral—"

"And don't forget that this is Jubilee Summer—the sixtieth year of the reign of Queen Victoria," Jeremy broke in, catching the spirit of the idea. "There should be some special events—parades and such, I'd think. Maybe they'll even be able to catch a glimpse of the old lady herself out in her carriage, reviewing her troops!"

"Well, it sounds like an exciting summer ahead," said Faith, finishing her coffee and standing up. "I'll be happy to help with the planning. Won't it be wonderful to see the cousins

again? I haven't seen the Bondurants, Lally and Lenora, since
... well, since Uncle Rod's wedding to Aunt Blythe."

"And we've never seen Druscilla's *own* little girl, Evalee,"
her mother reminded her.

"Nor have we met Jonathan and Davida's children," Faith
said as she came to drop a kiss on her mother's smooth cheek.
"I must go now, but we'll have plenty of time to discuss all
this later."

"Now, don't be too late, dear. You always come home so
worn out from your days at that place," Garnet said
petulantly.

"I'll try to be home early," Faith promised, giving her father
a hug. "Good-bye, Papa."

"Have a good day, dear girl," Jeremy said, clasping the
hand she put on his shoulder and giving it a reassuring
squeeze.

His eyes followed her as she left the room, thinking of what
a strikingly handsome young woman his daughter had
matured into—tall and slim, with glossy dark hair, and
bright, intelligent eyes, even if her chin was perhaps a trifle
too square for classic perfection. If only he could be sure she
was happy—

"I wish we could do something to keep Faith from
traipsing down to those awful slums and exposing herself to
who knows what!" Garnet said peevishly. "Sometimes I could
just wring Lydia Ainsley's neck for encouraging Faith in her
own particular brand of good works!"

"They do a lot of good, my dear. From what Faith tells me,
conditions are extremely bad for those people, the women
and children particularly. Why, I've heard that Lydia's friends
provide the only square meal that some of them get in a week.
Frankly," he said, squinting at her over his spectacles, "I'm
glad that our daughter has a compassionate heart."

Garnet's eyes widened and she drew herself up indignantly. "But, Jeremy, *we* do a great deal for the village people in Glenmere when we're down at Birchfields! Why, I'm always sending baskets of fruit and vegetables to the vicarage to be placed in the poor boxes. And sometimes I go with the vicar's wife and some of the others in the Ladies' Guild to visit the sick and poor. Isn't that enough?"

"You do your part, my dear, but you mustn't discourage Faith when she chooses to help in other ways," Jeremy remonstrated gently. "She isn't a child anymore, you know."

"Don't I know *that*? She's twenty-three and no nearer to being engaged than she was five years ago when she came out! I declare, I sometimes wonder at poor Neil Blanding's patience. He *still* has hopes, I presume." She let out a long sigh.

Jeremy folded up the newspaper that he had not had a chance to finish reading and rose from the table.

"Well, my darling, I must be off to the office. I have a new author to interview today before taking him to lunch at the club."

Walking over to Garnet, he looked down into her uplifted face, leaned down and kissed her tenderly, once, then again. Even after all these years, Jeremy still found his wife alluring and lovely.

"Have an enjoyable day, Garnet, love. I do think your plan for a family reunion at Birchfields during Jubilee summer is a capital idea."

After Jeremy left, Garnet remained at the table, working out the details of the marvelous plan she had devised. Absentmindedly, she started to take another slice of bacon but stopped herself mid-reach, giving a sigh of resignation. At forty-seven, one ought to be able to eat what one wanted without worry! But not with today's fashions!

The new "hour-glass" figure did not allow for a single extra bulge or an inch if one were to keep the "wasp waist" it decreed. Not even her daily horseback ride whether along London's Rotten Row or in the country lanes around Birchfields insured *that*. So she must watch the temptation to overindulge in fattening foods.

Resolutely, she pushed back her chair and stood up. While she was out riding this morning, she would think about the entertainment for her guests this summer. Soon she should be getting letters of acceptance from her brother Rod and Blythe, from dear Jonathan and his wife, Davida, at Montclair, and from Druscilla— Here, Garnet paused. Would Dru's husband, the aloof Randall Bondurant, agree to come to a family reunion? Maybe after all these years, he had decided to let bygones be bygones, although Garnet knew for a fact that his first wife Alair's parents, Aunt Harmony and Uncle Clint Chance, had never really forgiven him for, as they told it, "driving Alair to an early grave."

Ah, well, whoever came or did not come, she would make them all welcome and do everything possible to make this an unforgettable summer for everyone.

She picked up the *London Times* that Jeremy had discarded at his place, her eyes traveling casually over the page that he had folded back. Then she saw something that caught her attention—the lead in bold type of Grace Comfort's "Moment of Inspiration" column—and read:

We can make of our lives what we will, nettles and thorns that wound others—or give off a fragrance that beautifies and delights. Give and receive, share everything you have.

> Don't horde, or store, open both hands,
> Be joyously generous to what life demands,
> Sharing and caring, kindness and love

Are gifts to the soul from the Creator above.
Of your talents and abilities give the best.
If you are the giver, you'll be the blest.

"What drivel!" Garnet exclaimed as she flung the paper down in exasperation. "Now why on earth would Jeremy have circled this?"

chapter

8

Cameron Hall
Mayfield, Virginia

"WATCH ME, Mama, watch me!"—eight-year-old Scott Cameron, mounted on his gray Shetland, called to his mother, who was standing on the stone terrace steps.

"I'm watching, darling!" Blythe called back, exchanging a proud glance with Rod, who was standing alongside the boy and his pony.

"Ready, Scott?" asked his father.

"Ready," the boy replied, leaning forward.

Rod gave the pony a slap on its hindquarters, then stepped back as the pony started at a trot and headed toward the low hedge at the end of the lawn. As they took it easily, Rod shouted, "Good jump, Scott!"

Scott turned his pony around and trotted back.

"Now it's my turn. *My* turn, Papa!" Six-year-old Katherine tugged at her father's arm.

"All right, Miss Impatience, *your* turn." Rod laughed, turning to the little girl, who was jumping up and down.

"*No! It's mine! I'm* next, aren't I, Papa!" protested Carmella.

"Now, just a minute, you two," said Rod, casting a perplexed glance at his wife, who shrugged as if to say, "You deal with it."

"Here, I'll tell you what. Scott will get down, and Kitty can ride Doby this time, and Cara can take Cleo," Rod suggested.

"I want to have my own pony!" declared Carmella sulkily. "It isn't fair."

"But, sweetheart, was it fair that you rode your own pony too hard yesterday, and poor Clancy went lame?" her father reminded her. "Now don't pout. Look what a good sport Scott is to let Kitty ride his pony." Rod lifted his daughter up into the saddle of the other pony, a gleaming cinnamon color.

Carmella picked up the reins in small gloved hands but looked straight ahead, not down at her father.

"Scott, run down to the stable and get Jed to saddle Pacer for you to ride. We'll meet you down at the pasture gate."

Blythe silently complimented her husband on his diplomacy. For a man who had come to parenthood late in life, Rod was a devoted father who took obvious pride in his children.

Scott dismounted and set off at a run toward the stone stables visible from the house. Rod then swung his second daughter up into the saddle of the gray pony. Kitty straightened her shoulders, then cast a dimpled glance toward her mother.

Blythe clapped her hands and nodded approvingly to Kitty, at the same time glancing at Cara's stubborn little profile. How different their two daughters were, in spite of their being "mirror-image" twins—Kitty, right-handed; Cara, left-handed. Although physically almost identical, the two sisters could not have been more unlike in character and personality. Kitty, who had been named for Rod's late mother, Katherine Maitland, seemed to have inherited many of the qualities of her gentle grandmother. Cara was christened Carmella after Blythe's Spanish mother who had been a gypsy dancer whom she could not even remember. Was it possible that Cara's fiery temper, her independence, and tendency to dramatize herself came from this unknown source?

A moment later Rod mounted his own horse and, with a word to the twins, started along the drive to the place where Scott was to meet them at the entrance into the woods.

"Have a good ride!" Blythe called after them.

When the riders disappeared, she returned to her chair on the sunny veranda and picked up the letter she had left on the table when Scott summoned her to watch his jump.

It was from Rod's sister, Garnet, and Blythe reread it with mixed feelings. She and Garnet went back many years, not always pleasant ones. When Blythe had first come to Virginia as Malcolm Montrose's bride, she did not know that Garnet had been in love with him for most of her life or that the then widowed Garnet had hoped to marry Malcolm herself. After all, she had taken care of his invalid mother and his little boy, Jonathan, after the death of his first wife, Rose. Malcolm had been away, fighting with the Confederate Army. Afterward, still reeling from the tragic accident, he had fled to California, where he had met Blythe. When he returned home at last, bringing another bride, it was, in Garnet's mind, a betrayal.

Of course, that was all in the past. They were both now happily married for the second time, to devoted husbands. This scrap of history should not influence Blythe's decision to accept or refuse Garnet's gracious invitation to spend the Jubilee summer at her English country place.

Besides, it would be an unexpected opportunity to see Jeff, her son by Malcolm, now studying art in London. She had not seen him for almost two years. His last visit to Virginia had not been a particularly happy time, and she was eager to make amends.

Her husband, Jeff's stepfather, had not been pleased with her son's decision to drop his architectural studies at Oxford University to become an artist. When Rod had suggested that Jeff apply to the University of Virginia, hoping that the boy would eventually go into the Cameron family business of raising thoroughbreds, he was not the least bit interested.

"You'll have to wait for Scott, I guess" had been Jeff's indifferent response to his stepfather's suggestion.

Although Rod had not said much, Blythe knew that he disapproved strongly of Jeff's change of plans. To Rod, Jeff's artistic ambitions seemed impractical and foolish. But she was caught squarely in the middle between the two men she loved dearly. Defending one to the other was increasingly painful.

During his last visit to Virginia, Jeff had spent a great deal of time at Avalon in Arbordale, the home where he and Blythe had lived before her marriage to Rod Cameron. Although the house had been rented several times over the years, it was now unoccupied. Jeff would be gone for hours, riding on the bridle paths that wound through the beautiful woodland surrounding the island estate he had known as a boy, revisiting all his secret places, she learned later. He would return from these solo excursions, silent and thoughtful.

Blythe sensed Rod's resentment of the time Jeff spent at Avalon, even though she completely understood what it meant to her son. It was *his* property, and his affection for it bordered on the same kind of feelings that Rod had for Cameron land.

When he married Blythe, Rod had wanted to adopt Jeff legally, make him his heir. But at sixteen, Jeff had rejected the idea. He reminded his mother that he was a Montrose, with his own heritage, one as long and honorable as Rod's. In fact, the Montrose family had come to Virginia from Scotland at the same time as the Camerons. Although Jeff had been cheated out of his right to Montclair through Cousin Druscilla Bondurant's deeding it to Jonathan, Jeff's half-brother, *Avalon* belonged to *Jeff.*

It was with a measure of surprise and a great deal of satisfaction that Blythe had first recognized her son's strong family ties. She hoped that he would one day come back to Virginia to live. But while he remained in England, she wanted, *needed* to make this trip.

Blythe's close friends and Jeff's godparents, the Ainsleys, saw him often, and Lydia wrote that he seemed well and happy with his career choice. In Garnet's letters, too, there was a frequent mention of Jeff's visits to Birchfields and how fond they all were of him.

Blythe felt a twinge of jealousy. She envied both Lydia and Garnet for being able to enjoy Jeff's company, his dynamic presence. Quickly she rejected that emotion as unworthy. She ought to be glad that Garnet and Lydia welcomed Jeff so warmly and made him feel at home. But she could not shake the fear that he was beginning to feel more English than American.

That thought brought a sense of guilt. If he did, it was her own fault. Hadn't she fled to England after the shock of Malcolm's death and the loss of Montclair because of his gambling debt? Maybe that was why Rod never wanted to visit England again, since it was there that Blythe had hidden herself for so long. He had searched everywhere after she disappeared.

Blythe sighed. There were other reasons, too, why her husband might not want to go. If ever a man loved his own native land and birthplace, it was Rod Cameron. He had inherited Cameron Hall and its vast acreage from a long line of prestigious ancestors, beginning with the stalwart Scotsmen who had come to Virginia before the American Revolution to tame the wilderness. Until the birth of their little son, Scott, Rod had been the only remaining male descendant.

The more Blythe thought about Garnet's invitation, the more tempting it seemed. Garnet had assured her that Birchfields, with its twenty bedrooms and large staff of well-trained servants, was adequate for all the people she had invited.

Rod *must* agree to go to England for the Jubilee summer! It was Blythe's chance—and maybe her only chance—to try to recapture that precious closeness that she and Jeff had once shared. If any more time passed before they were reunited, it might be too late.

chapter
9

Hurricane Haven
The Bondurants' South Carolina Island Home

"OH, HOW LOVELY, Drucie!" exclaimed Lenora, who was the first to respond when Druscilla told them about Garnet's invitation. "When would we go?"

"May, I suppose." Dru glanced down the table to her husband, Randall Bondurant, for his reaction.

"And how long will we stay?" was Lalage's question.

"That depends. Aunt Garnet says most of the events celebrating the Jubilee will take place after the royal family returns from their holiday at Balmoral in Scotland. That's in August, she says—"

"Imagine! Seeing Queen Victoria in person!" declared Lenora.

"This is her diamond jubilee as monarch. That's why it will be such a festive season," Dru explained, scanning the letter for details.

"Jubilee summer! I love the idea!" sighed Lenora, then turning to her sister, she asked, "Don't you, Lally?"

"Who else will be going?" Lalage wanted to know.

"Aunt Garnet says she's written to Blythe and Uncle Rod and of course, to Jonathan and Davida, too."

"Will Jeff be there, do you suppose?" Lalage asked shyly.

"Aunt Garnet writes that she's invited all the family, so I'm sure he will be. He's in London now, I believe, studying art. But he comes down to spend the weekend occasionally at Birchfields with Aunt Garnet and Uncle Jeremy—" She paused, studying her husband's bland expression again. "So, Randall, what do you think?"

Randall lifted his dark eyebrows and gave an imperceptible shrug as he signaled to Jerod, the butler, standing at the sideboard, to refill his wine glass.

"I'm not sure that your Aunt Garnet's invitation to the family necessarily includes *me*, Druscilla, my love." There was a slight edge of sarcasm in his voice. "Surely you've not forgotten that I've never been completely accepted by your prestigious Virginia family, the Montroses and the Camerons, to say nothing of the Chances."

At this reminder of the heated controversy over Randall's first marriage to her cousin, Alair, and then the second series of shock waves that reverberated when *she* married her cousin's widower nine years later, Druscilla's cheeks flushed. But she dismissed his comment lightly.

"Oh, for pity's sake, Randall! All that was years ago, and besides—" Dru halted, inclining her head toward her two stepdaughters and their own eight-year-old Evalee, who was all ears by this time—"Perhaps we should talk about this later—"

Evalee, alerted by the interesting undercurrent to this conversation, glanced from her mother to her father and back again. "You mean, not in front of *me*, don't you, Mama?"

"Well, darling, there are many things to be decided before taking such a long trip. Going so far away requires a great deal of planning and arranging. England, where Aunt Garnet lives, is across the ocean and—"

Evalee tossed her glossy dark curls impatiently. "I *know!* I've seen it on the globe. Noey showed me, didn't you, Noey?" she demanded of Lenora, using the family nickname for her older half sister.

"Yes, I did." Lenora gave Dru an almost apologetic look.

"I want to go!" Evalee thumped a small fist by her plate, making the silverware dance. "Please! Do let's go, Mama, Papa! We'll get to travel on a big boat, won't we? And I'll get to sleep in a little bunk and all the windows will be round. . . . I've seen pictures in the 'cyclopedia—" Evalee bounced on her chair, nearly sending it tumbling backward.

"Whoa, little lady!" Randall held up a warning hand. "Nothing has been decided yet. Your mother and I have to discuss a great many things before we make any decision. How does this trip sound to you, Lenora?" He glanced at his eldest daughter, thinking with a sharp pang how very like her late mother she was. But she was, thank God, totally unlike Alair in character and personality!

Lenora faced him, her expression serene but her dark eyes shining. "Why, I think it would be wonderful, Papa! Such an education! To be in England for a historic occasion like Queen Victoria's Jubilee celebration. Imagine, she's reigned longer than any other living monarch. She became Queen when she was younger than either Lally or I."

Randall threw back his head and laughed. "Do I detect an attempt on your part to convince me that this trip would be an *educational* experience for my family instead of a frivolous social occasion?"

Lenora had the grace to blush. She darted a quick look at her stepmother, "Not exactly, but then—"

"Oh, Papa, we *must* go, we must!" Evalee hopped down

from her place and ran to the end of the table, where she threw her arms around Randall's neck. "Please, Papa, say we can go!"

"We haven't seen our Virginia cousins in ages, Papa," Lalage reminded him.

"The Cameron twins or Scott!" added Lenora.

"Nor Jonathan and Davida's children, Kendall and Meredith," Dru said.

"And I've never met any of them!" Evalee looked offended.

"That's because I'm the only one who went to great-Aunt Kate Cameron's funeral, dear," her mother said.

"It would be such fun, all of us aboard a ship bound for England!" sighed Lalage wistfully.

Druscilla laughed and raised her eyebrows imploringly as she looked to her husband once again. "I think you're overruled, Randall, dear. I believe I'm going to have to write Aunt Garnet and tell her we're coming."

"Well, you'd better tell her to rent us a cottage to ourselves. I doubt very seriously if Birchfields will be able to house this unruly bunch." Randall shook his head in mock despair as he glanced around the table at all the eager faces. But his smile told Dru they had won the day.

chapter
10

Montclair
Mayfield, Virginia

"DOESN'T THAT sound absolutely splendid, Davida?"

Lifting his eyes from the letter he had been reading aloud, Jonathan Montrose looked over at his wife seated across the breakfast table. *What a pretty picture she makes*, he thought as he waited for her answer, with the morning sun making an aureole of light around her soft brown hair.

Davida put down her coffee cup with a frown.

"But, Jonathan, of course we can't go!" she protested. "You *know* I promised Papa we'd spend the summer with him at the Cape. He's already seen about renting a house, and he's looking forward to it so much. It would simply break his heart if I didn't come and bring his grandchildren. You know how much he loves Kendall, and he's not seen either of them in almost a year!"

"There will be other summers, Davida," said Jonathan mildly, trying to be reasonable. But accepting his aunt's invitation was something he very much wanted to do, and he was prepared to risk an argument. "This will be an opportu-

74

nity for the children to be with their cousins and have the experience of a first trip abroad. Surely your father would understand. As Aunt Garnet points out, *this* summer is special. Not only because England will be celebrating the Queen's Diamond Jubilee but because all the family will be there—"

"All *your* family, Jonathan." Davida's reply was sharply sarcastic.

Startled by his wife's tone, Jonathan looked at her in surprise. "*Your* family, too, Davida," he remonstrated gently.

"But if we go to Massachusetts *as we planned,* Jonathan, you would be able to be with your Uncle John and Aunt Frances Meredith. After all, they were like parents to you. I should think you'd feel even closer to them than to your Aunt Garnet!"

"You must remember, Davida, it was Aunt 'Net who took care of me right after my mother died. I might have been just three years old, but I remember the security she gave me at that terrible time," he reminded her quietly. "She cared for me in every way a mother would, and she didn't want to give me up to the Merediths. She was simply complying with my dying mother's wishes in case my father didn't come back from the War."

"Your *father!*" exclaimed Davida indignantly. Clenching her hands, she looked away from the reproachful look on her husband's face.

She rose from her chair, went over to the window, and stared moodily out, oblivious to the elms greening on either side of the curving drive and the woods beyond, pink with dogwoods in bloom. "Your father—" she repeated, "was responsible for this mix-up! If he hadn't lost this place in a card game to Bondurant and then Druscilla deeded it back to you, we wouldn't even *be* here! We'd be living happily near Papa just as we planned!"

Jonathan looked shocked at his wife's outburst but kept silent.

Finally Davida spun around and faced him. "I'm not going and that's that!" she declared, stamping her foot. "I *won't* disappoint Papa. I'm all he's got. And if my being with him can give him some pleasure, then I intend to do it. *You* can go to England if you want to!"

"By myself? Without you and the children?" Jonathan's voice sounded as forlorn as he felt, remembering that other long, lonely time before Meredith was born, when Davida had gone north alone and stayed away for months and months.

Just then Matthew came into the dining room, bringing a silver pot steaming with fresh coffee.

"I don't want to discuss it just now," Davida said pointedly, nodding in the butler's direction as Matthew refilled both their cups.

Jonathan's mouth settled into a grim line. He knew that there was no use pursuing the matter in the presence of the servant, and sipped his coffee in silence. But inwardly he was torn. He did not anticipate with much pleasure the thought of accompanying Davida to the house his father-in-law had leased for the summer, of spending hours in polite attentiveness while Kendall Carpenter expounded his theories on the state of the nation and the world. Jonathan rarely agreed philosophically with the old gentleman anyway.

Furthermore, he was intrigued by Aunt Garnet's invitation to visit the Devlins' country home. Although he had often been urged to come, it had never worked out. Either Davida had been unwell in one of her several unfortunate pregnancies, or they had been committed to spending the summer at a place his father-in-law had ordained and arranged for them. Then there had been the births of their two children and the impossibility of traveling with babies. There had always been a hundred such reasons to refuse. But now he saw none that would prevent their accepting. Kendall was seven and Meredith nearly six, old enough to be good travelers and to enjoy the adventure.

It would be a treat to visit with many of the relatives he barely knew or had not seen since childhood. His cousin, Druscilla Montrose Bondurant, would be coming with her family, Aunt Garnet had written. But most of all, Jonathan viewed this as a chance to become better acquainted with his half brother, Jeff Montrose, the son of their late father Malcolm's second marriage to Blythe. Of course, she was now married to Jonathan's uncle, Rod Cameron, who had been their neighbor at Cameron Hall. The Camerons, of course, had been invited. Jonathan liked Blythe and admired Rod, and he had been particularly fond of Rod's mother, Aunt Kate Cameron, who had died a few years ago.

Yes, the whole idea of a family reunion in England appealed to Jonathan in almost every way. That's why this unexpected roadblock Davida had put up had met with greater resistance than usual. He did not know whether to back down, insist that his wife accompany him, or agree to the months of separation from Davida and the children.

Jonathan had learned through previous experience that an unwilling Davida was a coldly uncommunicative person. Only if things went her way was she the sweet, loving girl that he had fallen in love with and married twelve years ago. Beneath that soft, feminine exterior lodged a stubborn, willful woman. It wasn't all her fault, Jonathan told himself. After all, she had been pampered since babyhood. As a motherless child, she had grown up as her papa's spoiled darling, accustomed to having her way in almost everything.

Now, Jonathan feared, perhaps it was too late for her to change.

Almost from the first day they arrived in Mayfield, Jonathan had been made to feel guilty for uprooting Davida from her native New England and bringing her to Virginia when he inherited Montclair, the ancestral home of the Montrose family. Since then, Jonathan had found that giving in to his wife was often the price of domestic peace.

When Davida rose from the table, Jonathan followed her across the hall and into the drawing room, which Davida had completely redecorated upon moving to Montclair. It was handsomely furnished in the style of the times, with heavy carved furniture upholstered in dark velvet and a grand piano covered with a fringed cloth. Over the ornate mantelpiece was an almost life-size portrait of Davida's father, Kendall Carpenter, resplendent in the uniform of a Union Army colonel.

Whenever Jonathan looked at it, which was as infrequently as he could manage, he could not help thinking that his father, Malcolm, and his two uncles, Bryce and Lee, who had all served in the Confederacy, must be turning over in their graves!—to say nothing of his Grandfather Clayborn Montrose, who had refused to return to his native Virginia when it meant taking the Loyalty Oath after the War.

Jonathan closed the louvered doors behind him, then spoke in a low voice so as not to be overheard by the servants. "Whether you want to or not, Davida, my dear, we have to discuss our family's summer plans."

Davida took a stand in front of the fireplace under the portrait and turned to face her husband. "I've made up my mind, Jonathan. I will not disappoint Papa. We're all he has—"

At her words, a firm resolve hardened within Jonathan. If Davida didn't want to go, he would not insist, but why should he deprive himself of a summer with his own relatives? Why couldn't he for once, after escorting her and the children safely to Cape Cod, take a steamer from Boston and spend a vacation of his own choosing? As he considered it, the prospect seemed increasingly pleasant.

Part III
Voyage of Discovery

Aboard the Ruritania
Late Spring 1897

One of the pleasantest things in the world is going on a journey.

—William Hazlitt

chapter
11

ON SAILING DAY the staterooms of the *Ruritania* were abloom with flowers of every hue and description, while the ship's stewards were kept busy making deliveries through the crowded passageways. Every few minutes another bouquet arrived from some friend or relative, wishing the passenger a "Bon voyage!"

The adjacent doors of the Bondurant and Cameron staterooms remained open, and there was much traveling back and forth between the cabins and much sharing of congratulatory notes and gifts. Each delivery of a beribboned basket of fruit or elaborate box of candy was greeted by a shriek of delight from Evalee and ohs and ahs from Lalage and Lenora while Randall read aloud each telegram and card attached to the several gift bottles of champagne addressed to him.

"I didn't know we had so many friends!" exclaimed Dru as she opened still another envelope containing good wishes for their journey.

"Or so many admirers!" declared Lally mischievously as she handed Lenora a card that had accompanied one of the green florists' boxes.

Blushing, Lenora snatched the card from her sister, saying archly, "*You* should talk. I saw that woebegone expression on

Frank Clement's face when he came to see us off in Charleston!"

"It's like a party! *Is* this a party?" Evalee kept asking. "Is this really a party?" Her cheeks were flushed, her eyes bright, as she looked from her mother to her two older sisters flitting about the cabin.

"This is the first of many, many parties, sweetie!" Druscilla smiled and gave her a hug. "This whole summer will be one party after another!"

"Oh, good!" Evalee said, spinning around on her toes several times in the small space as Druscilla turned to direct the porters wheeling in the steamer trunks.

"Look, Lally, here's one for you—" Lenora read from the tiny card she had taken from the top of one of the florists' boxes: "He says he's going to miss you! I didn't know Bradley Farrington was sweet on you!"

Her pretty younger sister playfully snatched the card from her. Giggling, the two blond heads bent together over the long, white box, folding back the layers of green tissue paper to reveal dewy yellow sweetheart roses.

"Let me see! Let me see!" demanded Evalee, pushing her way between them to gaze into the box. "I wish somebody had sent *me* flowers! Or *candy!*" she said, her rosy mouth pursed in a pout.

"Don't worry, Evalee, by the time you're sixteen, you'll have dozens of beaux sending you bouquets and so many boxes of chocolates you'll be as plump as a pigeon!" Lalage told her, winking at Lenora over the little girl's head.

"I don't want to be *plump!*" Evalee retorted.

"Oh, honey, Lally was just joking." Lenora brushed back the dark curls from the brow of the frowning upturned face. "But not about the beaux. You'll be sure to have plenty of those!"

"Well, well, it sounds like the party's in here!" said a deep male voice, and they all three turned to see a tall, smiling man standing in the door of their stateroom.

"Jonathan!" cried Druscilla and rushed forward to embrace him.

With one arm still around his waist, Dru looked into his face. "So you couldn't persuade Davida to come with you?"

The brown eyes regarding her affectionately darkened. "No. She didn't want to disappoint her father. There was nothing I could say to change her mind."

*   *   *

The first night at sea, dress for dinner was informal. But the second night, it was understood that in First Class, shipboard protocol demanded that evening dress was *de rigueur*. The Bondurant party was scheduled for the second seating, and for two hours beforehand, Lally and Lenora were in a flurry deciding what they would wear.

Once it had been decided that they would make the trip to England, Dru had seen that their new wardrobes included a half-dozen evening dresses for each of them. "I'm sure Aunt Garnet has lots of parties planned for this summer, and I want you both to do your father proud," Dru had told them, knowing that Randall took enormous pride in his two pretty, older daughters.

The result of Dru's wise planning was evident in Randall's pleased expression as he extended his arms to escort his daughters into the mirrored elegance of the main dining room that evening. And Dru, following with Jonathan, was aware of many heads turning in the direction of the two tall, slender blonds as they found their table.

As they were being seated, Dru had a small nagging concern about her youngest daughter, Evalee, who was becoming more and more of a problem. Earlier, the child had put up a fuss about going with their stewardess to dine with her younger Cameron cousins. Only the promise of the puppet show, a special entertainment arranged for the children afterward, had headed off a threatened tantrum.

Well, she wouldn't worry about that tonight, Dru decided. She was determined to enjoy herself and this wonderful trip with its chance to be with Jonathan, her favorite cousin. It would be the first time they had had any real time together in years—actually, since they both had married. And now they will have the fortnight it would take them to reach England.

Dru looked across the table at Lenora and Lalage. Both young women were flushed with excitement, their great dark eyes shining with delight as they took in everything about them. It made her smile just to see them so happy. *This trip will be a wonderful experience for them, something they will remember all their lives*, Dru thought.

Their stepmother was not the only one observing the Bondurant sisters with more than casual interest. One diner, in particular, found his attention riveted on them.

Victor Ridgeway, seated at a table opposite, lingered over his coffee and cognac, watching them discreetly. From his vantage point he had a clear view of the serene profiles, the sweep of blond hair caught up from the slender column of their necks. Enchanted, he could not take his eyes off them. One of them was especially stunning. *Only the words of a famous poet could adequately describe her golden beauty*, he thought: *"A daughter of the gods, divinely tall, And most divinely fair."* Who were they and how could he persuade the captain to introduce him?

At the Bondurant table, Lally nudged Lenora and whispered in her ear. "Don't look now, but right across from us is the most divine man staring at us!" She squeezed her sister's arm. "He has such brooding eyes. Oh, my! He is so romantic looking!"

Accustomed to her sister's enthusiasm, Lenora's gaze followed Lally's nod. There he was—a distinguished looking gentleman seated alone. His dark hair was cut close, defining a well-shaped head. And his eyes *were* marvelous. A narrow beard outlined a firm, strong jawline.

Just then those eyes caught and held hers. For a moment she could not draw a deep breath. She felt a tingling coursing through her body, and the color rose into her cheeks. As she looked away quickly, Lally sighed.

"I wish there were some way we could meet him."

The girls never expected that opportunity to come so soon, nor did they expect that it would change their lives forever.

*   *   *

"There he comes now!" hissed Lalage, clutching Lenora's arm just after they settled into their lounge chairs the next day.

Lenora recognized the man strolling toward them as the same man to whom she had had such a strange reaction at dinner the night before. Now at his approach, she was experiencing the same breathlessness. Flustered, she ducked her head over her book, and scolded, "For goodness sake, Lally! Don't be so obvious!"

"He's stopping at the rail right in front of us!" Lally informed her in an excited whisper. "He's looking out at the ocean!"

Lenora forced herself to keep her eyes on her book. But after reading the same sentence over for the third time, she gave in to her curiosity and lifted her eyes to look at him for herself.

It was just as Lally had said. He had paused at the railing as if to contemplate the sun shining on the water, calm as glass, on this third morning at sea. Of medium height, he had a lithe, trim build. He had looked quite splendid in dinner clothes but was equally striking, she thought, in the tweed Norfolk jacket and matching visored hat he was wearing today.

As she was making this survey, he turned and looked directly at her. A slight smile touched his lips as he raised his hand and tipped his cap, nodding before he moved on.

"Who do you suppose he is?" Lally exclaimed when he was out of sight. "He's obviously traveling alone."

"How do you know?"

"That's easy," Lally said. "He was sitting at a table for one last night. So that must mean he's not married."

"Not necessarily," Lenora said cautiously. "Jonathan's traveling alone and he's very much married—"

Ignoring her sister's remark, Lally hurried on. "I think he's a bachelor, or maybe a widower with a tragic past."

"Oh, Lally!" Lenora had to laugh, knowing what a romantic her sister was. A devotee of Brontë novels, she was prone to give people dark histories and secret tragedies.

"Well, anyway, I wish we could meet him," said Lally plaintively.

Sooner than either of them could possibly have imagined, they did. The very next day, while strolling with their parents on A deck, they came face-to-face with the gentleman in question in the company of the ship's captain, and introductions were made all around.

Later, in the privacy of their stateroom, Victor Ridgeway became the main topic of conversation. Lally was ecstatic.

"Did you hear his accent? So very British—so definitely upper-class. Why, he's probably of the nobility or most certainly of the aristocracy. Victor Ridgeway—" she repeated the name, drawing out each syllable. "He must be of a very fine old family, one with a country estate or an old castle or a manor house that's been there for generations—" Lally's voice drifted off dreamily.

That evening as the Bondurants were having their after-dinner coffee in the lounge, Victor Ridgeway himself entered and their father waved him over to join them. Although Randall and Mr. Ridgeway monopolized most of the conversation, Lenora found herself drawn to the melodious voice, the warm, intelligent eyes—

"I understand you have just made an extensive tour of the United States," their father was saying.

"But only the northeast and west," Victor corrected him almost apologetically. "I'm afraid I missed the southern states and historic South Carolina—a pleasure, I understand, that I should not forego next time I visit your country."

A few more pleasantries were exchanged before Mr. Ridgeway moved on to another table.

But the following day, as the girls joined other passengers routinely strolling the decks for exercise, they encountered Victor Ridgeway again, this time alone, and this time it seemed perfectly natural to stop and chat with him.

He fell into step beside them and afterward sent a note to Druscilla's stateroom, inviting her and the two young ladies to join him for tea in the First Class lounge. It was then that his warmth, pleasant personality, and interesting conversation won over their stepmother completely. They learned that he was widely traveled and had spent several winters in Italy, so they found much in common, since the Bondurants had lived near Rome when the girls were younger. Later, Dru commented favorably on Mr. Ridgeway's intelligence and charm.

Every afternoon thereafter, it seemed entirely natural that Victor should join the family for strolls on deck or engage with them in other shipboard activities, such as shuffleboard and quoits. And it became almost a daily event to have afternoon tea together and share after-dinner coffee in the lounge.

Of course, Evalee was sometimes around, and Lally, being the one most easily persuaded to "play" with their younger sister, often went off with the child, frequently leaving Lenora alone with Victor. Since he was at least ten years older than she, Lenora was surprised that they quickly found so many mutual interests.

They talked for hours about books, music, poetry. Before long, Lenora, always shy, found herself sharing more of herself than she ever did with anyone other than very close family members. It had all happened so quickly, so naturally, that even Lenora did not realize just when their friendship had deepened into love. Not until the morning of their sixth day at sea, when she answered the steward's knock and was presented with a single white rose and an envelope containing a note addressed to her.

"A thing of beauty is a joy forever, Its loveliness increases—" from "Ode on a Grecian Urn," Keats

First glance, first word, our first hour together will remain a shining memory pressed to my heart. Like a lovely flower, it will always retain its sweet perfume.

> Yours devotedly,
> Victor Ridgeway.

As she read it, Lenora's cheeks flamed and her heart thudded crazily.

"What is it, Noey?" her sister asked curiously.

"It's a flower, a rose—" She held it up, then put it to her nose, inhaling its fragrance. Then, eyes, wide with wonder, she turned to her sister. "And . . . a note . . . from Victor Ridgeway."

"From Victor Ridgeway?" The younger girl paled. "For *you?*"

There was something in her sister's voice that tugged at Lenora's heart, and she turned a stricken look on her. "Yes . . . Oh, Lally, I'm sorry! I never meant . . . I hope you didn't . . . Here, you read it," she faltered, handing the note to Lally.

Lalage's expression underwent a series of changes, from interest to disappointment, and at last, resignation. Then she looked at Lenora, her eyes huge. "You realize, don't you, that Victor Ridgeway is in love with you?" she demanded. She shrugged and gave a rueful smile. "And just when I was hoping *I* could be the one. Well, I guess he couldn't be in love with *both* of us!" The usual mischievous twinkle returned to her eyes. "I'm sure he had to draw straws to decide which of us it would be!" Then she laughed and gave her sister an impulsive hug. "I'm glad for you, Noey. Besides, I was too young for him anyhow!"

chapter
12

SINCE RANDALL BONDURANT had come into her life, first as her employer after she accepted his offer to become governess to his two daughters, then as her husband, Druscilla had become a world traveler. Always a keen observer of people, she could not fail to notice Victor Ridgeway's increasing attentiveness to Lenora.

Having been the witness to many "shipboard romances" that ended abruptly once an ocean liner docked in port, Dru was wary. She did not want Lenora to be hurt by the older man's flattering attention. Dru was afraid that, in her inexperience, the young woman might mistake it for more than it meant.

Yet, as she continued to watch the relationship develop, what had at first appeared to be only a brief romantic attachment for the duration of the Atlantic crossing became much more. At length, Dru felt she must discuss her concern with Lenora's father.

"Randall, I really need to talk to you about something," she said one day as she entered their stateroom after breakfast and her morning stroll.

A look of impatience crossed her husband's face. "Can it

wait, my dear? My bridge partner is waiting for me in the salon."

By the third day at sea, Randall had found three other avid card players and had initiated a daily game. Although he had long ago given up gambling as a profession, Randall enjoyed the skill and competition of the game of bridge, just now coming into popularity.

"It's important. At least, I believe that it is." Dru's brows furrowed in concern. "It's Lenora."

"*Lenora?*"Randall looked surprised.

Of his three daughters, Lenora was the one least expected to cause a problem. Indeed, she had never given them a moment's worry. Now, if Dru had said Evalee, that would have been an entirely different matter. His youngest was a little minx, with the promise of turning her parents' hair gray in the years ahead. But Randall did not want to contemplate that—not just yet.

"Yes. Lenora," Dru repeated. "It's about—Victor Ridgeway. Well, I think . . . I suspect . . . actually, I'm *sure* he is quite smitten with Noey and . . . well, he's much too old and sophisticated for her!" Dru finished breathlessly.

"What makes you come to such an astonishing conclusion?"

"Why, it's obvious! At least, to *me*. He can't take his eyes off her, he follows her every move, he hangs on her every word, he takes every opportunity to be near her. He walks when she walks, he accompanies her to her deck chair, he manages to be at the tea table when she arrives—oh, any number of things tell me it is true!"

"Well, has he behaved in an unseemly manner, taken any advantage—?"

"No, no, of course not. Mr. Ridgeway is a perfect gentleman. A perfect *English* gentleman, which adds all the more appeal to his attentions. Our girls are quite sheltered, you know. We live so simply on the island, with no social life to speak of, except when we go to Charleston at Christmas time to stay with your mother and sisters. But Lenora has no experience with the likes of Victor Ridgeway—" Dru hesitated, struggling to put her vague uneasiness into words.

"Besides, there's some mystery about him," she continued. "Nothing I can put my finger on, but he is treated with such deference by the officers and crew, even Captain Streicher, almost as if he were—I don't know—*somebody*."

A suspicion of a smile curved Randall's mouth. "Somebody? My dear, *everybody* is '*somebody*'."

"Oh, Randall! Don't mock me. You know what I mean! He is forming a . . . an *attachment* to her!"

"So what do you want me to do about this so-called 'attachment,' which I must say—" Here Randall paused, regarding his wife with outright amusement— "seems a most *unnatural* attraction. I can't imagine why a vigorous young man with two good eyes should notice a beautiful young lady!"

"Don't tease, Randall. This is serious."

"My darling wife, I don't agree. I don't think it's at all serious. Certainly nothing for you to be upset about. Listen, we are fewer than four days away from England. This *attraction* that worries you so much can last only a few more days at most. Once we dock, we whisk our daughter away to the English countryside, where your aunt has promised to supply her with all manner of proper young British blades nearer her own age. No doubt, some of them will be equally smitten, as you call it, with the lovely Lenora. So, for goodness sake, put your mind to rest and concentrate on keeping Evalee out of mischief—a much more worthwhile occupation, if you must worry about something."

With that, Randall crossed the room, took Dru's face in both hands, and kissed her long and thoroughly. When she opened her eyes, he was smiling down at her.

"Now, go enjoy your day. This is a wonderful chance for you and your cousin Jonathan to have a nice leisurely visit— one I know you've been looking forward to for a long time. And now I must go. Wish me luck and a good hand. Arthur Pelham is a wicked opponent."

After Randall left, Dru gave a long sigh. She hoped her husband was right. That there was really nothing to worry about. Maybe she *had* overreacted. But there was something about Lenora—a certain distant look in her eyes, except when she was in Victor Ridgeway's presence, when she came truly alive. In Dru's opinion, her stepdaughter's glow was more than the effects of the invigorating sea air!

Dru sighed again and picked up her mohair shawl. She had better hurry or she'd be late for her daily deckside stroll with her cousin. Her visits with him had been delightful, if somewhat unsatisfactory. Something was troubling Jonathan. Maybe, before long, he would tell her what it was.

* * *

As Dru came up on deck, she paused for a moment before she caught sight of Jonathan. He was leaning on the railing, his head turned to study the horizon, where the deep blue sky met the foam-flecked ocean swells.

In that unguarded moment, Jonathan looked vulnerable, sad, even melancholy. He *was* keeping something from her! The easygoing manner he had adopted since setting sail on this trip was only a facade. Why hadn't she noticed the signs of strain, the lines around his mouth, the deep unhappiness in his eyes?

Unaware of her presence until she touched his arm,

Jonathan turned quickly to greet her. But for a split-second before the smile came—the endearing, boyish one—Dru could read the tragedy in his face, and it wrenched her heart.

"Dru! Good morning!" He tucked her arm through his as they began to walk.

After a few turns around the deck, Jonathan showed no signs at all of dropping his determined air of cheerfulness. But the fact that only three days remained before reaching their destination gave Dru the courage to blurt out the question she had been wanting to ask from the first.

"Are you happy, Jonathan?"

He looked startled but recovered quickly. "Why, of course! Why wouldn't I be? Seeing you again, Cousin. Fine accommodations, superb cuisine, excellent companions. Even the weather has cooperated in giving us a perfect crossing."

"Oh, Jonathan, that isn't what I meant! It's just that I want so much for you and Davida to be happy. I had hoped that having Montclair—your rightful heritage—would give you a good start. Was I right?"

Jonathan patted her hand but didn't reply right away. Finally he pulled her into a sheltered passageway.

"You're wondering if you did the right thing deeding Montclair back to me? It was such a generous thing to do, Dru, and so like you to do it. And I appreciate Randall's sensitivity to our family as well—and yes, it did make me very happy—"

"But?" she persisted. "I feel there is an important 'but', Jonathan."

"Dru, I hope you'll understand what I'm about to say." "Try me."

"I could be completely content, Dru. It's Davida. I've tried everything to please her . . . and I guess I just don't know how to make her happy—" he trailed off miserably.

"You can't *make* someone else happy, Jonathan," Dru said gently.

"I know that but . . . well, you see, she never really wanted to move to Virginia . . . away from her father. She agreed only because she thought it was expected of her—" Jonathan paused again, looking out toward the ocean, dark blue now and sparkling with sunlight. "It hasn't worked out, Dru. Each year when she goes to visit her father in Massachusetts, she stays away longer and longer—"

Dru felt a rush of sympathy for her cousin but could think of nothing to say to comfort him.

"I don't blame Davida," Jonathan continued earnestly. "You see, her New England roots go very deep." He shook his head. "If Davida could have found a friend in Mayfield, perhaps she could have made the adjustment more easily. But she complains that Southern women are different from her friends in the North, and I suppose she's right—"

He turned to Druscilla. "You have to understand Davida's background, Dru. You've heard of the Peabody family of Salem, haven't you? Elizabeth Peabody is famous throughout New England for her progressive educational ideas, especially in the education of women. Davida attended Elizabeth Peabody's school."

He sighed. "Well, Davida says she just doesn't fit into our way of life in Virginia. She doesn't ride, thinks fox hunting is barbaric, and won't even attend the social events held during that season!" Jonathan shrugged. "Honestly, Dru, I don't know what to do. Somewhere along the way . . . we seem to have lost each other."

Dru sincerely wished there was something she could say to help. But what would that be? She herself understood too well the sad consequences of marrying someone with an

97

entirely different background, set of values, thought, and philosophy.

Her mother, Dove Montrose, had warned her about marrying Randall: "You don't just marry the *man*, dear, you marry the *life*." Dru had not been able to change Randall. He still gambled occasionally, though not recklessly, the way he used to. But he had never been able to resist the thrill of taking a risk, of trying to win against all odds. Her mother had been right. It was useless to marry someone, expecting to change him . . . or her. One should marry for love, then be prepared to take the bad with the good.

She knew there were things in her own marriage that could not be shared, things she and Randall never talked about. She had wanted so much to give her husband a son, someone to carry on the Bondurant name. She had suffered the heartbreak of a stillborn child with her first pregnancy, then two subsequent miscarriages before their daughter was born. Then she had been told that there would be no more children, and this had been the cruelest hurt of all.

Each marriage had its own secret sorrows, she knew, so although Dru could sympathize with Jonathan's particular burden, there was nothing she could do to assuage it.

He took her hand again and pressed it. "Come on, let's not be gloomy. I didn't mean to burden you with all this. Look, here come Blythe and Rod—if ever there was a happy couple, *they* certainly seem to be. Let's go join them."

* * *

"Isn't it too bad Davida and the children couldn't come?" Blythe was saying to Rod as they walked briskly toward Dru and Jonathan.

"*Couldn't,* or *wouldn't?*"

"What do you mean?"

"From what I gather, without Jonathan's being specific about it, his wife preferred spending the summer with her father to making this trip."

Blythe looked at her husband in surprise. "You don't think she *wanted* to come?"

"That was my impression."

Blythe's hand tightened possessively on Rod's arm. "I can't imagine being separated from *you* for months."

"You and I have had enough separations to last a lifetime," he said quietly. Then he added, "If you really want to know what I think, it's that Davida is not very happy in Virginia, at Montclair. And, of course, that means Jonathan is not all that happy, either."

"Oh, I hope you're wrong, Rod! What makes you think so?"

"Just a feeling—" He smiled ruefully. "I know, I know. Women are supposed to be the intuitive ones. But Davida has appeared restless to me from the first time I saw her again after they moved to Montclair—a totally different young woman from the happy bride I met at their wedding."

"But Jonathan is the perfect husband—kind, considerate, loving—" protested Blythe. " What makes you think she is restless?"

"To be truthful, it was Mother who noticed it first and brought it to my attention. She remarked on very much the same things you've said. How could Davida be unhappy when she has everything any woman could want—beautiful home, a caring, affectionate husband, children?"

"The same things *I* have, all of which make me sublimely happy!" exclaimed Blythe.

"That's just it. There seems no visible reason and yet, there it is. I think she is so attached to her father and her own family ties that she simply could not make the transition to another kind of life."

Blythe considered this possibility for a moment. "I suppose I should understand that. I was desperately unhappy when I first arrived in Virginia from California—"

"But that was entirely different, my dear. Your circumstances were not in the least like Davida's," Rod reminded her. "Come, let's not dwell on the past—it's too painful for both of us. Let's just do what we can to make Jonathan's summer without his wife and children as happy as possible."

Joining Dru and Jonathan, the two couples strolled the length of the deck, keeping their conversation lively as they anticipated their family reunion in England.

But Blythe could not put thoughts of Davida Montrose out of her mind. This shipside lull in the busy routine of her life had given her rare time for contemplation. For one thing, it was good to see her stepson again. She had not known Jonathan as a child since he had grown up in Massachusetts, reared in the family of his mother's brother, John Meredith. In fact, she had not even met Jonathan until he brought his own bride to be the new mistress of Montclair.

Blythe had liked him on sight, though she had been startled by his resemblance to his father, Malcolm. His gentle spirit and courteous demeanor reminded her of the man Blythe had married out West. But when she and Malcolm moved back East, her husband's personality had quickly disintegrated. Their marriage had never been the refuge that Blythe, as an orphan, had expected and needed. Nor was there much visible support from the Camerons, whose plantation adjoined Montrose land.

It was only much, much later that she realized how much her neighbor, Rod Cameron, had guessed about her tragic life with Malcolm, and how much he had come to love her.

Blythe reined in her wandering thoughts. What was to be done about the young couple whose love seemed to be dwindling?

Perhaps when they returned to Virginia in September, she could help Davida in some way. At least she would make a real effort to become friends, to see that their children, all of nearly the same age, got to know each other better. Surely there must be something she could do. Who knew better than she what it is like to feel lonely and isolated?

chapter
13

THE MEETING HOURS for the Sunday morning religious services on board were posted on the ship's *Bulletin of Daily Events*. A Catholic Mass was to be celebrated at nine, and a non-denominational service was scheduled for eleven in the main salon on A-Deck. The latter was to be conducted by the Reverend Mark Dennis.

At quarter to the hour, the Bondurant family joined the Camerons already seated in the row of chairs placed in a semi-circle around the large room. With a rustling of her apricot taffeta skirt, Lenora settled herself between Lally and Evalee, conscious that Victor had come in only minutes behind them and had found a place at the back.

Her heart began fluttering strangely, and she hoped his presence would not distract her during the service. Quickly she closed her eyes and prayed for composure.

When she opened them, the Reverend Dennis was standing at a podium up front. To her surprise, she recognized him as the same young man that she and Lally had often seen striding briskly on deck. In his cable-knit, roll-necked sweater, his sandy hair tousled and his face ruddy from the sun and wind, he looked more like the athletic coach of a college than a minister of the Gospel. W   nora felt a pinch on her arm, she knew Lally was hav   same startled reaction.

Without risking a sidelong gla   r sister, Lenora tried to concentrate on what Reverend   s was saying.

"First I would like to say how very   I am to have the opportunity to hold this meeting. On t   second Atlantic crossing, I am as much in awe of God's   cent creation as I was on the first trip. More thrilling   may I say, *humbling*, is that this is the first time I ha   asked to conduct a Sunday service on board.

"You may find this an unconventional place fc   hip—no stained-glass windows, no kneeling benches, no   ar. And the fact is that those of us gathered here probably represent a half dozen or more denominational backgrounds. Still, we are here for the purpose of glorifying God together, so as unorthodox as it may seem, this is holy ground.

"In England, you will be seeing churches of every description—from great cathedrals to small ivy-covered chapels. But when you enter the church of St. Clement's Dane in London, you will see the following sign:

WELCOME TO GOD'S HOUSE, WHOEVER YOU ARE, OF OUR HOUSEHOLD OR OF ANOTHER FAITH OR A WANDERER OR A SEARCHER. BE WELCOME HERE. PRAY FOR US, AND FOR ALL SINNERS, ALIVE OR DEPARTED, THAT GOD'S MERCY MAY DRAW US ALL ONE SMALL STEP NEARER TO LOVE'S UNVEILED AND DAZZLING FACE.

"This morning I welcome you to this unique hour of worship. The Lord Jesus Himself has said, 'The time is coming when true worshipers will worship the Father in Spirit and in truth.' Wherever there is a hunger and thirst for the living God, whether in humble cottage or vaulted cathedral or on a ship in the Atlantic Ocean, there is true worship.

103

"Join with me in singing the beautiful hymn, 'Amazing Grace,' for it is surely by His grace that we are all here this morning."

From a corner of the room, where one of the ship's officers was seated at a small organ, the haunting melody of the beloved hymn rose in tribute to the one God who brings all believers together in unity.

Then Reverend Dennis led them in a Communion service, reminding them that the taking of the bread and wine was commonly held to be the same enriching ritual for all believers, and all were invited to partake.

"Let us go now in peace and take the Lord's blessing with us throughout the rest of the day," the Reverend concluded. "Wherever we go on this ship, whomever we may come in contact with, let us remember that we have all been created in the image of God to praise and worship Him and to love one another."

Lenora felt deeply moved by the sincerity of the minister's words, and her heart lifted in response to the call to a common sense of awe at God's majesty. In fact, she couldn't help thinking that before Dru had come into their lives with her deep faith and loving example, there had been no one to point them to God. She felt a rush of gratitude at the thought of all she owed her stepmother.

In spite of herself, Lenora felt an irresistible urge to turn her head slightly and in so doing met Victor's penetrating eyes. With the impact of his gaze strong upon her, she caught her breath.

Then the service was over, the spell broken. Dru was touching her arm and Evalee was tugging at her sleeve. As they merged with the other passengers lining up to speak to the minister, Lenora lost sight of Victor. Had he slipped out?

The room was abuzz with conversation as people chatted

about plans for the rest of the day, and the stewards moved among them, serving coffee. Lenora smiled woodenly and spoke when she was spoken to. But the room seemed empty to her without the one person who was missing.

The next morning Victor's note accompanying a white rose confirmed her belief that they had shared the same reaction to the Sunday service:

"Beauty is Truth, Truth, Beauty, That is all we know on earth, And all we need to know." Keats. How wonderful that when we cannot find the words to express our deepest feelings, God has inspired the great poets and scribes of the ages to do it for us. I thank God for the miracle of meeting you, knowing you—that is a part of His truth for *me*.

Ever devotedly, Victor.

Lenora was glad that Lally had already left their cabin to take Evalee to breakfast and that thus she was alone to read what Victor had written. She and her sister had always been so close but—this was different. Was *this* love? Could it have possibly happened to her, this unexpectedly, this soon?

chapter
14

THE LAST NIGHT on board before landing in England, a gala costume ball was to be held. Since it was to be a masked affair with no one revealing his identity until midnight, there was a great flurry of discussion over what disguises would be worn.

"What fun!" exclaimed Lally excitedly. "But whatever shall we wear?" she asked Lenora, not knowing that her sister already had an idea.

The only problem with Lenora's plan was finding the costume she had in mind. It was one of Victor's daily notes that had planted the idea in her head:

My dear Lenora,

Sometimes I feel like the legendary "Harlequin," the poet who, in love with the fair Princess Columbine, disguised himself as a clown. Feeling unworthy to approach her or reveal his feelings, he loved her from afar. And so he wrote poems and left them in the palace garden for her to find. Dear heart, read between these lines and imagine why I place myself in the role of the unfortunate Harlequin.

Later that same day, when Lenora had met Victor on deck for their usual stroll, she had tried to reassure him that the distance he imagined between them did not exist. But he had simply shaken his head.

"You are too young, too naive, or maybe just too American to realize it, Lenora. I am sure, however, that your father and stepmother would agree with me."

"Please don't say that, Victor!" Lenora protested.

"We won't talk about it any more if it makes you unhappy. Let's just enjoy what time we have left—"

Lenora, however, was troubled. That is why the idea for her costume seemed so appropriate. When Victor saw her in it, he would know that their ages, their nationalities, his sophistication, her inexperience—none of these made any real difference.

Of course, in the end, Lenora had to confide in Lally and they went together to the ship's costumer for help. There was a wide selection of costumes to choose from, and although Lally found one right away—a bright Indian sari, trimmed with an ornate gilt border—Lenora took longer. Having consulted the ship's library earlier, she had found a picture of Columbine in a book about operas, filled with sketches and photographs of the leading ladies known for various roles. Under the heading of "Italian Opera," she had read the story of "Pallachio," a variation of the classic romance of Pierrot and his hopeless yearning for an unattainable love.

With that picture firmly in mind, Lenora searched through the racks for a garment she could adapt to the character of Columbine. Among them, she came upon a ballerina costume. Layers of white net billowed out from its fitted black satin bodice into an ankle-length skirt. In a box of accessories, she found black lace mitts, satin dancing slippers, and a mask beaded with sequins and trimmed with maribou.

"You must pull your hair straight back and into a rounded

club at the nape of the neck, then tie it with a bow as the French dancers do," instructed the costume lady.

When she tried it on later before the mirror, Lally, enthusiastically entering into her sister's scheme, clapped her hands. "On you, Nora, that style is so becoming! But only a person with dainty ears and a perfect heart-shaped face could get away with it!"

When Dru looked in on them before the party, however, she seemed a little startled by Lenora's choice of costume and tactfully suggested a wide black velvet ribbon for her neck and a lace scarf to cover her bare shoulders.

When they went into the Grand Salon for the ball, they found the ballroom extravagantly decorated with colorful streamers floating from the chandeliers and balloons sailing on the ceiling. Almost as soon as Lenora entered the room, she saw a Harlequin and her heart almost stopped. It was Victor, who had even shaved off his beard to enhance what he had hoped would be the perfect disguise. His trim build complemented his black-and-white diamond-patterned costume, complete with black net ruff, velvet tricorn hat, and black mask.

How extraordinary and yet how understandable that Victor would choose the very character in which he has placed himself, Lenora thought. His eyes met hers and instantly, irresistibly they moved toward each other. He bowed before her and held out his hand and, before she knew it, she was in his arms on the dance floor. They moved effortlessly, as if buoyed by invisible wings.

It was an evening that spun and shone with brilliant clarity, yet everyone and everything else blurred into an obscure haze in the background. Only Victor's eyes behind the black mask was etched in her memory.

At fifteen minutes before midnight, Victor took Lenora by

the hand and led her through the passageway up onto the deck. "I have to talk to you alone, privately," he had whispered, much to her bewilderment, since they had been dancing together almost exclusively all evening.

Up on deck Lenora saw other couples who had fled the crowded ballroom to stroll arm in arm or to sit, heads close together, for a moment of quiet conversation. Victor found a secluded corner and, leaning on the rail, he stared out at the glimmering, moonlit ocean. When at last he spoke, she was surprised at the tremor in his voice and the apparent agitation in his manner.

"My dear Lenora, I have something of great importance to say to you and I don't really know how or where to begin."

She felt her heart thudding. "But what on earth could you tell me that would be so shocking?" protested Lenora, not sure she was ready to hear. "Since I've come to know you, Victor, there's nothing you could say that would alter my feelings—"

"Then I've misled you. Oh, not intentionally. But by what I've done over the years before I met you, before I dreamed anyone like you existed . . . or that I'd ever be lucky enough to find someone like you—so unspoiled, so sweet—"

"But, Victor—"

"Please, my darling Lenora, listen to me before you say another word. First of all, I am *not* a gentleman." He heard her gasp and waited for his first shocking statement to settle in her mind. "Oh, I pass for one, and most people are kind enough to consider me one . . . but I come from the part of society that knows nothing about country weekends, hunting, dinner parties, or fancy dress balls. Would you believe I learned all that . . . from my *valet*? Yes, a man who had worked for a member of Parliament, whom I wooed away from his former employer with the offer of an extravagant salary. It was this 'gentleman's gentleman' who taught me how to disguise myself as a gentleman. But down deep inside, I remain the cocky cockney who dropped his 'h's' and didn't know a teacup from a tea cozy!"

Lenora started to say something, but Victor wouldn't let her interrupt.

"So, you see, I'm a fraud, my dear. Not in your class at all."

Before Lenora could protest, Victor caught her hands and clasped them tightly.

Then, before either of them could speak, Lally's voice broke in. "Noey! Come! They're about to give prizes for the best costumes, and they're calling for Columbine and Harlequin. Come along, you two, you've won!"

* * *

Lenora rushed through her packing and, leaving Lally to hunt for missing odds and ends, hurried up on deck, looking for Victor. Last night, after they had been awarded their prizes for the most original costumes, they had been surrounded by admiring people offering congratulations and compliments on their clever idea. Later they joined the other prizewinners at a special table where a sumptuous midnight supper was served. There Dru and Randall, with Lalage, had stopped by to escort Lenora back to her stateroom. There had not been another minute all evening to be alone with Victor.

Lenora had awakened early. She was dressing quietly so as not to disturb the still sleeping Lalage when the steward had rapped at the door and left Victor's usual offering. Today his note accompanied a small package containing a tiny sterling silver cornucopia pin, holding a white rosebud. The words he quoted from Tennyson held an ominous note of finality that frightened Lenora.

Their meeting made December June,
Their every parting was to die.

Surely, he wasn't saying good-bye! Surely he didn't think they would never see each other again! She must find Victor and ask him to explain.

Arriving on deck, Lenora realized they must already be docking, for passengers were crowded two deep at the rail. England! They were landing, and there would only be a half hour at most for her to find Victor, talk to him, make plans—

She quickened her pace, scanning the crowd, searching for that familiar figure, hoping he might be looking for her, too. The crowds thronging the passageways and decks increased until Lenora felt the huge ship shudder as its hull scraped the side of the dock and eased into the slip. Hordes of people eager to disembark were pushing toward the gangway, while those who had been waiting for the travelers to arrive were hurrying up on deck to meet them. It was impossible!

Lenora heard her name called and whirled around to see Lally, holding onto her hat, being jostled and elbowed as she made her way toward her sister.

"Noey, where have you been?" Lally sounded exasperated, "Everyone's been looking for you! Drucie was frantic and Papa was getting very annoyed."

"I was—" started Lenora, who then decided that there was no point in trying to explain, since her search had been fruitless anyway.

Somehow she had missed Victor. He had not given her his London address although he knew where to find her, knew that she would be spending the summer at Birchfields. Still, his strange outpouring to her the night before had filled her with uncertainty. What had he meant? Would she ever see or hear from him again?

111

"Oh, look, there's Uncle Jeremy Devlin!" exclaimed Lally, pointing to a tall, distinguished-looking gentleman with dark hair silvered at the temples. He was standing at the top of the gangplank in earnest conversation with another man.

Following the direction of her sister's pointed finger, Lenora felt instant relief. The man Jeremy was talking to so intently was *Victor*. She broke away from Lally and started to push her way toward the two men, but before she could reach them, they shook hands. Victor tipped his hat and, followed by his valet who had been waiting behind him, was immediately swallowed up in the crowd surging down the gangplank.

Lenora halted, dismayed. Why hadn't Victor sought her out to say good-bye? She touched the small silver pin on her dress lapel under her coat. Surely he would get in touch with her—and since he seemed to know Uncle Jeremy—

So many questions rushed into Lenora's mind, yet one constant remained. She was sure that Victor loved her, and she knew now that she loved him. This just could not be the end of the most thrilling, the most important thing that had ever happened to her!

Part IV
Jubilee Summer

In England
Summer 1897

I sing of brooks, of blossoms, birds and bowers—
Of June and July flowers.
Of bridegrooms and brides—

—Robert Herrick

chapter
15

ALMOST FROM the moment she set foot on English soil, Lenora felt a sense of homecoming. Although she had not been here since she was a little girl, it seemed as if everything had a familiarity about it.

Maybe it was because this was Victor's birthplace—the city he knew, as he said, like the back of his hand. He had told her about his apartment in London and that he was looking for a place in the country, somewhere peaceful and serene where he could write.

So, approaching Birchfields, Lenora's first thought was how much Victor would love it. As they left the quaint timbered train station and drove through the village with its cluster of small gray stone cottages, his presence seemed to hover everywhere. Passing a picturesque, ivy-hung church, they started down the winding country road to the Devlins' house. June roses in riotous bloom tumbled over meadow walls and fences. She inhaled deeply, thinking that never again would she be able to smell that strong sweet perfume without Victor's image flooding her senses. *Victor, Victor, where are you?*

When she saw the house—its gabled roof, the diamond-paned windows, the yards of velvety lawn stretching out to the graceful birches growing along the riverbank—it, too, seemed strangely familiar. *This would be the kind of place where Victor would like to live*, she thought, adding, *And so would I.*

What bliss it would be to walk beside that river, hand in hand with him, hearing his rich, mellow voice reciting poetry: "Come live with me and be my love"—

They had talked much of poetry, of books they had read, paintings they admired, music—and their own thoughts. He had never seemed a stranger, not even from the beginning. In fact, it seemed most unusual how soon she had known that she loved him. Despite his latest revelation, she had sensed in him a depth of thought and emotion, a tenderness of heart and spirit that had drawn her to him. It was a rare thing in any two people, she felt sure, but to find it in someone of such disparate background, experience, and age . . . well, this must be a miracle!

Yet how could she tell anyone that she had fallen desperately in love with the discreet and elusive Victor Ridgeway? What would her parents say, especially her father? And who would believe that someone like Victor could love *her* in return?

She touched the small silver cornucopia pinned to the inside of her jacket lapel, not wishing to show it to anyone yet nor to have anyone question her about it. Not even Lally. She glanced at her sister with a twinge of guilt. Lally hadn't guessed her real feelings for Victor, nor had she told the younger girl about their midnight kiss on the deck the night of the costume ball.

Uppermost in her mind, however, was when . . . or if . . . Victor would try to get in touch with her. Had she given him the address of the Devlins' home in the country? Everything had been so rushed, so confusing those last few hours, she could not be sure. All she knew for certain was that she was in love—deeply, ecstatically, completely in love—for the first time . . . and forever.

Lenora's private worries were temporarily forgotten as they entered the front hall of Birchfields. Paneled in dark, polished oak, the hall gave way to a wide stairway leading upward from a pair of heavy, carved posts. A huge fireplace whose hearth must surely beckon with roaring fires on a blustery winter evening, now displayed a large blue-and-white vase holding purple hydrangeas.

On the walls the portraits of bewigged gentlemen wearing ruffled jabots glared down out of their ornate frames at the intruders.

"They came with the house!" Garnet explained airily. "So we left them up. They add a touch of English aristocracy, don't you think?"

"What a magnificent place, Aunt Garnet," Lenora said, looking around, though she could not help thinking how very different was this Tudor mansion from their home on the beach in South Carolina with its wrap-around veranda, its windows looking out to the sky and sea, its feeling of openness.

On the contrary, this brooding house held a hint of tragedy. Her aunt's next words confirmed her first impression.

"I don't know all the details, but this house has a dark history. The former owners told us that there is supposed to be a secret room somewhere, a place where fugitive priests were hidden during Cromwell's time when Catholics were persecuted in England. But they could never find it. And neither could we—" She laughed—"although I believe Faith and Jeff have searched for it many times!"

As if by magic, three young women in frilly white caps and aprons appeared, and Garnet directed them to take her guests to their rooms. The one assigned to Lenora and Lalage, a pretty, pleasant girl named Annie, bobbed a little curtsy and led the way upstairs.

"I'm really Miss Faith's maid," she told them, as she opened the door to a spacious room with flowered chintz curtains at the windows and twin brass beds covered in the same matching fabric. "But I'm to help you ladies while you're here. There's the bellpull right beside the fireplace." She pointed it out. "It rings down in the servant's hall. If you want anything I haven't seen to, all you have to do is pull it." She stood and looked about with a frown, as if checking to see if everything was in order, then gave a nod and quietly left them.

Lalage, looking at her sister with eyes twinkling, clapped a hand to her mouth to suppress a giggle. In the Bondurant family, with only four house servants and a cook, no one had a personal maid! In fact, at Hurricane Haven, her father and Dru insisted that the household should be run casually and without fuss. So this would be a unique experience.

Lenora shrugged and flung out her hands. "So . . . when in Rome?"

"Oh, Noey, *this* is going to be such *fun!*" Lalage sighed happily and pirouetted across the room.

Lenora had to agree that it was certainly promising, but she was still preoccupied with Victor and how he would get in touch with her so as not to raise eyebrows or questions.

This worry was quickly put to rest when a few days later a package arrived, addressed to Dru from Victor, containing a book and a note in which he expressed pleasure in having met her and the Bondurant family on board ship and the hope that their paths might cross again. Would Dru be so kind as to allow Miss Lenora to accept his small gift on the subject they had discussed often when he had the pleasure of her company? It was all very proper, and Dru could see nothing untoward in either the note or the gesture.

The title of the gift book was innocuous enough—*A Collection of the Best-Loved British Poetry*. However, Lenora did not share the note she found slipped between the pages, as if marking the Shakespearean sonnet that began: "Shall I compare thee to a summer's day? Thou art more lovely—" Nor did she show anyone the inscription he had written on the flyleaf: "I remember the way we parted, the day and the way we met—Ever devotedly, Victor Ridgeway."

She slipped the note into her pocket to read again in the privacy of a special place she had found—the maze of boxwood in the Devlins' garden:

> As I write this, sweet Lenora, I am in turmoil. My mind bids me be sensible. My heart tells me you will respond to what I say. The dream planted in my soul when we met is so special that I hardly dare put it into words. If there is a possibility that our friendship holds something deeper for you as well, will you write and let me know the true feelings of your heart? If I have misread them, simply do not reply—I will understand. Just know I shall never forget you.

Lenora's heart leaped as she read Victor's words over and over. She felt like shouting, like singing, like doing a thousand ridiculous things that a proper young lady would never think of doing! Victor loved her! Victor Ridgeway— man of the world, handsome, sophisticated but sensitive, and kind as well—really loved *her!* She had not dreamed it!

But what now? Of course, she would respond to his note. But how? What would she say? If she told him how she *really* felt—Lenora put both hands up to her flaming cheeks. A whole world of possibilities swung open to her, a world she had barely imagined!

Quickly she folded the note and tucked it into the bodice of her dress, next to her heart. Later, when she was alone in her room, she would think through her reply to him.

chapter
16

WITHIN A SHORT time the guests at Birchfields had settled into a pleasurable routine. There was never any lack of something to do—an expedition to view some historic site, winding paths to stroll, a leisurely game of lawn tennis or croquet with other houseguests. Or, if one were so inclined, one might paddle a canoe on the quiet lake or retreat to a hammock under a shady tree for reading or a discreet nap.

The summer could not have turned out more happily as far as the children were concerned. This could be attributed in large part to Phoebe McPherson, the delightful young Scotswoman that Garnet had hired as their temporary nanny for the summer. Glowing with vibrant health and energy, she had a lovely smile and the tiniest burr in her speech that immediately inspired the children's loyalty and their parents' confidence.

To Dru's immense relief, Phoebe's way of making everything seem an adventure succeeded in causing Evalee to give up her high-and-mighty "I'm too old for this" stance and join Scott, Kitty, and Carmella on many an outing.

Even though she adored her daughter, Dru had begun to recognize some deplorable traits in the little girl. While Evalee still had a child's natural charm, she was beginning to develop an art of manipulation that concerned her mother. What she had previously acquired through tantrums and naughtiness, she now tried to gain by resorting to more subtle tactics, so it appeared to Dru.

"That Miss McPherson is remarkable," Dru said to Jonathan one morning as they sat on the terrace, watching her with the four children.

"Yes, indeed," agreed Jonathan, wishing with all his heart that his own Kendall and Meredith could be enjoying her blend of magic—getting the children to behave in acceptable ways while still having much light-hearted fun.

"She's quite intelligent and independent," Dru told him. "From what she tells me, she has goals and ambitions beyond her present position as a governess. In fact, she is thinking of emigrating either to Australia or the States. More opportunities for women there, she says."

"What kind of opportunities? Marriage?"

He gave the young woman in question a long appraising look. Even from this distance, Miss McPherson, rosy-cheeked from the game of tag she was playing, presented a very appealing picture.

"No, I don't think so. She says she has heard that women may own property, buy land, that sort of thing. She said she's even read about women ranching in the American West!"

Jonathan let out a low whistle. "Well then, I would say she's quite a different sort of young lady indeed."

Dru laughed. "Of course, that could all change if the right man comes along, I suppose. I think of my own days as a governess. As you know, I married my employer!"

"Yes, but that was quite different. Besides—" Jonathan smiled—"I think Jeremy Devlin is out of the running. Incidentally, doesn't Aunt Garnet look splendid? She ages hardly at all," he commented, just as their aunt's tall, slim figure appeared at the terrace entrance.

* * *

It was several days later before Jonathan had occasion to become better acquainted with Phoebe McPherson due to a chance encounter in the downstairs hall. He was looking through the mail to see if there just might be a letter from Davida when Miss McPherson came down the stairs.

"Good morning," he greeted her.

"Good morning, sir. Has the post come?"

"Yes, and I hope you'll be luckier than I," Jonathan said with a slightly rueful smile after failing to find any mail from Massachusetts.

"Oh, I wasn't expecting anything. Just wanted to drop off a letter to go," she told him. "I'll just leave it for the afternoon pick-up." She placed an envelope on the silver platter at the end of the table, then turned to go.

She looked so bright and cheerful, and since he was feeling sorely in need of some cheering up, Jonathan indulged his curiosity about this self-assured young woman.

"So what adventure are you off to today with your charges?"

She seemed surprised at his question, since none of the children were his. "Why, we're off to the village fair. I suppose you don't have them in America, because Scott and Cara and Kitty say they've never been to one."

"Oh, but we have circuses and exhibitions and centennial celebrations—"

"Yes, of course. And the British and the Scots have their own, too, like the highland games. A village fair is very different from all that, but lots of fun with booths, games of chance, a merry-go-round, all kinds of food—"

"Sounds grand!" Jonathan interrupted. And after only a moment's hesitation, he added wistfully, "You wouldn't be needing some help in keeping those youngsters out of mischief, would you?"

Miss McPherson darted a quick curious look at him. "Are you suggesting, sir, that you might want to accompany us— me and the children—to the fair?"

"Well, yes, actually. Why not?" Jonathan was smiling widely now. "I was thinking particularly about Evalee. She's apt to be—"

At the wry expression on his face, Miss McPherson laughed. "You're welcome, then, if you'd like to come. I know the children would be pleased. We'll be leaving in about half an hour. I've permission to take the pony cart."

Jonathan felt his spirits lift immediately, and he took the stairs two at a time to change into something more appropriate for the day's outing.

When the party from Birchfields arrived in the village, the fair was already in full swing. The children were wildly excited, and Phoebe had reason to be grateful for Jonathan's gentle but authoritative manner. They decided to explore first and made the rounds of all the booths to see everything that was offered before choosing the activities they most wanted to do. Then, while eating an ice, each child named a first choice, and the others agreed to wait their turn. The whole affair was settled amicably, on the whole, and without too much argument or debate.

Phoebe gave Jonathan an admiring look. "You're very good with them. Have you children of your own then?"

"Yes, two—a boy and girl—about Scott and the twins' ages."

"And why aren't they with you for the summer, like the others?"

"They're . . . with their grandfather in Massachusetts."
Phoebe's eyes softened sympathetically. "Their mother's dead?"

Jonathan flushed. "Oh, no, she's . . . Davida's very much alive."

When Phoebe looked puzzled, he felt he must offer some explanation. "It wasn't possible for her to come with us . . . this time."

Fortunately, the awkward moment ended when he was called upon to arbitrate a small difference of opinion between Scott and Evalee.

"She's so bossy, Uncle Jonathan," Scott grumbled, not satisfied with the resolution. "Evalee's the bossiest girl I know. Girls shouldn't always get their own way, should they?" he demanded, scowling.

Jonathan, thinking of another young woman who most certainly or nearly always got her way, shook his head. "Well, I guess a gentleman just has to be patient and hope they'll come around, Scott."

Over the boy's head, Jonathan met Phoebe's serious gaze before he looked away.

Later, while all four children rode the merry-go-round, Jonathan and Phoebe strolled by the booths circling the carousel. Just as they drew abreast of the gypsy fortune-teller's tent, a swarthy man wearing a bandanna and with a gold hoop in his ear began hawking customers for "Salvana, the Seer," who waited inside.

"Come on in, lady!" He beckoned to Phoebe. "Salvana can tell you everything you wanna know—past, future, secrets of the beyond—"

"Want to have your fortune told, Miss McPherson?" Jonathan asked jokingly.

"*Me, sir?* I should say not!" Phoebe drew herself up with a show of indignation, although her eyes twinkled merrily. "I was raised strict Methodist chapel, Mr. Montrose. My old auntie would be scandalized at the very thought. Besides, I *know* my past, and I've planned my future quite carefully. I certainly don't need some gypsy fake telling me a lot of nonsense!"

"And what is that, Miss McPherson? Your future plans, I mean?"

"Well, I'm planning to move to America or Australia—I'm not yet sure which it will be. I suppose it depends upon what presents itself in the way of employment."

"That shouldn't be difficult. You're a very fine governess, Miss McPherson. Anyone can see that."

"Oh, but I don't intend to be a governess all my life, sir. In England, especially, such a position is very ambiguous—" She gave him a sidelong glance as if to gauge how much she should reveal. "You're neither part of the family nor accepted by the servants as one of them. One's status in a household is a kind of in-between space, you see. Highly uncomfortable, I must say. I guess I'm just too independent for that."

As the calliope music ended and the merry-go-round slowed to a stop, so did their conversation. In another minute the children were back, surrounding them and clamoring to try the penny-pitch for prizes, or visit the bakery manned by the Village Women's Institute, which offered luscious home-made pastries and cakes.

When the children began to get tired and cranky, Phoebe suggested it was time for them to pile into the pony cart and head back to Birchfields. Despite the busy afternoon with four energetic children underfoot, Jonathan was surprised to find that it had been his most enjoyable day since coming to England.

Of course, he missed Meredith and Kendall. And Davida,

too. But then, this was not the kind of outing Davida would have chosen. Subconsciously, he looked over at Phoebe McPherson, who was singing along with the children some uproarious nonsense song and having the time of her life!

chapter
17

GARNET, dressed in a tan poplin riding habit, was waiting for Rod at the bottom of the staircase. She smiled up at him, and for a second Rod was transported back to his boyhood days when his little sister had ambushed him to go riding with her. *From a distance, Garnet still looks about eighteen,* he thought fondly.

It had been three years ago, at their mother's funeral, since Rod had last seen Garnet. But his first thought had been how little his sister had changed. Her hair still shone with its burnished golden sheen, and her figure was still slim and graceful. In some ways she was even more attractive, he thought, her features softer, her expression mellowed by her leisurely lifestyle and happy marriage.

Now she tucked her arm through his and said in a stage whisper, "Isn't this delicious, slipping out before anyone else is awake and begging to go with us? I wasn't sure we could get away without *your* twins, who are obviously 'Papa's girls' and avid riders, from everything I've heard."

A look of pride crossed Rod's face. "Sleeping like tops, both of them, when I peeked into their room. I think that going to the fair yesterday exhausted them completely."

"This is just like the old days, isn't it?" she asked as they left the house and started along the path toward the stables.

"Not quite." Rod shook his head. "If *I* remember correctly, Stewart and I used to try to avoid our little 'tag-along.' To slip away, we'd even climb out our bedroom window onto one of those wonderful old oak trees at Cameron Hall. Then we'd sneak down to the stables, saddle up, and be off before you were awake!" he retorted, referring to the strategy he and his late twin had devised.

"Humph! Typical older brothers!" declared Garnet indignantly.

"I don't know how typical, actually. I notice that Scott takes quite an indulgent, protective attitude toward *his* little sisters."

"What a fine family you have, Rod. I'm so happy for you. You and Blythe seem ideally suited." Garnet studied his face, then asked with sudden insight. "You *are*, aren't you? Happy, I mean?"

"Oh, yes! Blythe is a wife any man would be proud and happy to have. The only thing—" he hesitated.

"Yes?"

"As you might guess, we do have some differences where Jeff is concerned."

"Oh, yes. Jeff. Malcolm's son." Garnet nodded. "Is that the problem? That he's *Malcolm's* son? Or is there something else?"

"You know I wanted to adopt him when Blythe and I married. I wanted him to be my son legally and in every other way. But he refused. Since he was nearly seventeen at the time, I certainly couldn't force the issue. Until then, I had not the slightest idea that he felt so strongly about his heritage . . . about being a Montrose."

"Did Blythe object or did she encourage the idea?" Garnet was curious.

"Neither, really. She remained neutral about the whole thing . . . which is her usual position in matters concerning Jeff." Rod slapped his riding crop against the top of his boot. "Sometimes I wish she would just say how she really feels—" He paused. "Five years ago, when he dropped out of school and went off to Europe, she agreed it was blamed irresponsible. But after her first shock, she took his part. Anyway, what could we do? At twenty-one, he came into his own money." Rod stopped short on the gravel path and faced Garnet. "An artist, of all things! Can you believe he wants to spend his life painting pictures?"

"He *is* very talented, Rod," Garnet murmured.

"Talent be hanged! Is that any way for a real man to occupy his time?"

Because Rod felt deeply about the issue, she knew it was useless to pursue it. So she took another tack. "You know he confided his plans to Faith, and she supported it and kept it from us," she told him. "I was very upset, you may be sure! But Faith says Jeff has always been interested in art, that as a boy he was always drawing and sketching—he just didn't make a great show of it. She says Jeff told her that he studied architecture as a compromise between what he really wanted to do and what might be considered acceptable."

Rod's jaw was set stubbornly, and he made no comment.

"I believe, Rod, that Jeff very much wanted to earn your approval," Garnet went on gently, "but came to a point when he felt he had to go his own way—with or without it."

"Well, he's gone *without* it, I can tell you that!"

By this time they had reached the stables, and the groom was leading out their mounts—Garnet's glossy-coated chestnut, Lady, and a sleek black horse with a white star on his nose for her brother.

"Let's don't talk about it anymore now," she suggested. Rubbing the mare's nose affectionately, she brought some lumps of sugar from the pocket of her jacket. "It's such a beautiful morning—let's not spoil it."

Rod did not reply. But as they rode out into the misty morning, he could not put out of his mind the question Garnet had posed.

Was it because Jeff reminded him so much of his father, Malcolm Montrose, that their relationship was thorny? The boy's resemblance to Rod's close childhood friend was uncanny. The three of them—he, his twin brother Stewart, and Malcolm—had grown up together on neighboring plantations. They had been inseparable, riding pell-mell through the woods around Montclair, hunting and fishing, doing all the things boys do when they are young and carefree.

And then the War had come. Everything had changed then. Stewart, killed in the first year. Malcolm, taken prisoner by the Yankees. Rod, too, had suffered a severe wound. But it was Malcolm who had changed most after the War. Reeling from the South's losses, he had been devastated by the death of his wife, Rose Meredith, in a tragic fire. When the War ended, Malcolm had gone to California. And when he returned, he had brought back another young bride—Blythe.

Remembering, something hardened in Rod. Was it Malcolm's treatment of Blythe that had somehow influenced Rod's feelings for their son, Jeff? Or was it his own guilt? Even while Malcolm was still alive, Rod had fallen helplessly in love with Blythe—his best friend's wife! But his code of honor had kept him from telling her or anyone else. He had loved her passionately, if silently, and had suffered with her as

Malcolm slowly deteriorated and eventually destroyed himself.

Then Blythe had disappeared, and it had taken Rod ten years to find her. By then, she had borne Malcolm's son and was rearing him by herself in England. Her whole life centered around him.

Marriage to Rod had meant a great deal of adjustment for all of them. Perhaps more for Jeff than for anyone else, Rod mused. He had a real live stepfather instead of a dead idol he had never known. And not only did he have to share his mother with another man but eventually with a half brother and two sisters. Yes, the boy had suffered, perhaps more than anyone knew.

Rod squirmed uncomfortably, thinking of the frequent clashes of will and temperament during the years that Jeff had been with them at Cameron Hall. He would be the first to admit that he did not understand the young man that Jeff had become.

In spite of the exhilaration of the ride, Rod's mind was still troubled. He loved his stepson and wanted a good relationship with him, but he was not looking forward to their first meeting in over two years.

*   *   *

The afternoon following their excursion to the village fair, Jonathan was seated at his desk in one of the guest bedrooms, trying to compose a letter to Davida. He had just begun when he heard the sound of merry voices and laughter on the lawn below.

Putting down his pen, he went to the open window and, when he looked out, saw Dru, Miss McPherson, and the Bondurant girls struggling to erect a net for a game of badminton. They were not making much headway and kept dissolving into giggles as each attempt to secure the net only succeeded in one end or the other's drooping lopsidedly.

"Need some help?" Jonathan called down to them.

Looking up, Dru placed her hands on her hips. "Whatever gave you *that* idea?"

"Quite frankly, I can't imagine!" Jonathan replied, laughing.

"Come on down then, and we might even let you join the game!"

Leaving the unfinished letter, Jonathan left his room and sprinted down the steps and out onto the lawn. When the net was tautly anchored, Miss McPherson offered to be score-keeper since the others were new to the game, one that had not yet gained the popularity in America that it enjoyed in Britain.

They commenced with much trial and error and a great deal of hilarity. Finally, Dru gave up, volunteering to take Miss McPherson's place with a rule book to help her keep score, and Phoebe became Jonathan's partner against Lenora and Lalage, who had quickly caught on to the game.

Miss McPherson proved herself to be a skillful player, and the Bondurant girls went down in defeat. Just as they called "Game!" the young people looked up to see the maids sent out by Garnet, bringing trays with a pitcher of chilled lemonade and a plate of wafer-thin English "biscuits."

"Wonderful!" exclaimed Lalage, flopping into one of the wicker chairs. "I'm dying of thirst!"

"I'll pour," offered Phoebe, filling a tall glass and handing it to her. "And here's another for you, Miss Lenora."

"Thank you. But, Phoebe, please call me "Noey." Most everyone does."

Jonathan saw Phoebe's thoughtful expression as if she were considering the suggestion, but he also noticed that she did not take Lenora up on the more familiar term as the conversation turned to a discussion of the game.

"I really like badminton," declared Lalage. "It's much less strenuous than tennis."

"Yes, and much easier. The rackets aren't as heavy, for one thing," Lenora agreed. "Phoebe, tell us, how did you get to be such an expert player?"

"Maybe it's because I had two brothers and had to be fairly good at all sports to keep up with them."

Jonathan would have liked to follow up on this remark, but just then Garnet came out on the terrace and started across the lawn toward them.

To his surprise, Phoebe put down her glass and rose to her feet, saying shyly, "I must go see about the children." With that she left, passing Garnet with a deferential nod on her way to the house.

Jonathan thought that her departure was abrupt, when they were all having such a pleasant time. Then he remembered what Phoebe had said about the status of governesses that day at the fair. No doubt, the approach of her employer had reminded Phoebe of her position at Birchfields and had precipitated her hurried leavetaking. Jonathan found himself resenting the situation without understanding exactly why.

He knew only at some deep, almost subconscious level that he was intrigued with Miss Phoebe McPherson. There was so much more he wanted to know about her.

chapter
18

By the end of the second week, Faith had nearly given up hope that Jeff would come down. Blythe, who had stayed a few days in London, visiting Jeff before joining the others at Birchfields, had explained that he was hard at work on a painting that he wanted to enter in an exhibit and did not want to leave unfinished.

On Friday morning, however, while Faith was helping her mother with the daily flower arrangements, Garnet made an off-hand remark. "Oh, by the way, remind me to tell Polly to get the bedroom in the east wing ready. Jeff sent word he'd be down on the 4:20 this afternoon."

At the mention of Jeff's name, Faith's color deepened, but Garnet, busy with the centerpiece, did not notice.

Jeff is coming! Faith repeated over and over to herself as she went to give her mother's instructions to the upstairs maid. She felt almost weak with excitement. Ridiculous, maybe. But it had been weeks since she had seen him. Jeff was more and more occupied, obsessed even, with his painting. But now he would be here for the whole weekend and it would be like old times, Faith thought happily—long walks, long talks, time alone, together—

Faith had hoped that she might meet Jeff at the station in

the pony cart, but Garnet told her that Clarence had already been dispatched to do some errands and would be in the village to pick Jeff up when his train got in. So in spite of her determination to remain calm and composed, Faith found herself running to the window every few minutes before tea time to see if there were any signs of the carriage.

When her vigil was finally rewarded, she brushed past Hadley on his way to open the front door and flung it wide just as Jeff alighted from the small trap.

"Jeff!" She raced down the steps to greet him. "I'm so glad you could come down!"

Her hand tucked into the crook of his elbow, she led him through the house, chatting all the while. "It's been much too long. You're pale! No doubt from working too many long, hard hours in that stuffy old studio. What you need is a weekend of fun and sun."

Jeff grinned down at her. "So look who's giving orders. You always were a bossy little baggage."

"Well, someone has to look after you. I don't know what Aunt Blythe is going to say when she sees you looking so peaked."

Jeff wrinkled his face into a worried grimace. "I've already been read the riot act about eating better and sleeping eight hours and getting out in the fresh air." Then he grinned. "So how are Mother and Uncle Rod enjoying the bucolic life?"

"Fine. Mummy's taken them to the local flower show, then on to meet some friends this afternoon, but they'll be back in time for tea.

"Having our cousins from America here has been marvelous," Faith told him as they went out onto the terrace. "And Neil Blanding has been over much more than usual, too."

"Maybe he enjoys playing croquet!" Jeff joked, seeing the lawn set up with everything in place for the game.

"Or maybe it's because the Bondurant girls are so much fun!" She laughed. "I don't see Lalage right now, but—come on," she said, tugging his arm. "I'll introduce you to Lenora." Faith pointed to a girl sitting on a rustic bench under one of the stately silver birches.

As they approached, Lenora stood up, and Faith thought the tall young woman looked more charming than she had ever seen her, in a blue voile dress and a leghorn picture hat, its crown wreathed in blue cornflowers. The shadow of the brim fell on her face, enhancing the delicacy of her features, the clarity of her complexion.

"Jeff, this is Lenora Bondurant," Faith introduced them. "Lenora, meet Jeff, your Montrose cousin."

"Hello, Jeff," Lenora said and held out her hand.

For an instant, Jeff was speechless. This lovely girl was most surely what the pre-Raphaelites called "a stunner." Her exquisite figure and features—the fawn-brown eyes with long, curling lashes, the creamy magnolia complexion, the silvery-blond hair—was the kind of perfection they had all searched for and glorified in their allegorical paintings.

She would be ideal for the painting he planned of Guinevere, the physical personification of the picture he had already formed in his mind. More than that, she had a kind of inner radiance that he knew instinctively would translate to canvas as a spiritual aura.

In the brief silence that followed, Faith read Jeff's expression as he gazed at Lenora and immediately knew what he was thinking—knew he would like to paint her! Nor could she resist thinking, *Oh, to have Jeff look at me like that!*

At last he managed the semblance of a greeting. "Hello, I'm—I'm happy to meet you."

"But we have met before."

"No!" Jeff protested. "We couldn't have. I would have

remembered, I'm sure. . . ." He studied the purity of her face, the sculpted features.

Lenora insisted, "Oh, yes, we have! It was at my mother's wedding, wasn't it?"

Jeff protested, "But that's been ages ago . . . ten years at least! You must have been only a little girl then. You've changed a great deal, or I couldn't have forgotten—"

"I've grown up, I guess."

"Yes, of course, that's it." His eyes moved over her, appraising, admiring. "You've become beautiful—quite beautiful."

As a peachy blush rose into Lenora's cheeks, Faith risked another look at Jeff and felt a sharp twinge and a sudden, awful premonition.

*   *   *

A moment later, Neil Blanding and Lalage, her bright golden hair tied back with a blue ribbon, appeared on the path leading up from the lake.

Much to Neil's disappointment, Evalee had insisted on tagging along with them. He had hoped to have some time alone with the beautiful American girl without her little sister's overhearing every word.

Neil found himself experiencing a whole new set of emotions ever since the first night he'd been invited to Birchfields to meet the Devlins' American cousins. His reserved English nature had been turned upside down after only a few minutes with Lalage Bondurant. He had found her not only immensely attractive but sweet and amusing as well, with none of the artifice that was so boring in some of the debutantes his mother had thrust his way. In contrast, Lalage was completely natural and delightful.

As she looked at him now with questioning eyes, he

137

suddenly realized she had asked him something and he had been so intent on his own thoughts that he had not heard what she said. Actually, it didn't matter, for Evalee had caught sight of Faith.

"We've been feeding the swans!" the little girl called excitedly.

Then, seeing that the croquet wickets had been set up and the mallets brought out, she began hopping up and down, first on one foot, then the other. "Can we play croquet now, Faith? Can we?"

"Yes, yes, of course," Faith replied as with effort she turned her attention from Jeff to her other guests.

With Neil's assistance she organized everything, handing out mallets as they chose teams. She tried to focus on the game as it got underway, but her gaze kept straying to Lenora's graceful figure as she swung her mallet. Jeff's eyes, too, seemed fixed on her.

Faith went through the motions, but as if from far off, the voices and laughter scarcely penetrating the feeling of imminent doom that hovered like a dark cloud over her.

Then quite suddenly, she noticed a kitten at the edge of the lawn. Unaware of the danger of the rolling balls whacked with force, the little animal ventured across the path of the game. Before Faith could act, Lenora dropped her mallet and ran to scoop up the kitten, resting her chin on its head. She cuddled it on her shoulder, rubbing its furry softness against her cheek.

Faith didn't miss the look on Jeff's face as he witnessed this touching tableau, his eyes following Lenora as she carried the kitten to safety then returned to the game.

The sun shone golden on the grass as the afternoon took its pleasant, leisurely pace. For Faith, who longed to escape the sight and sound of Jeff's and Lenora's teasing exchanges as they played, the hours seemed endless. She deliberately concentrated instead on the copse of birches beyond the velvety lawn where their game went on and on. Ironically, however, the wind sighing through the graceful branches only reminded her of Lenora's hair waving in the summer breeze.

chapter
19

WHEN IT WAS mentioned one evening at dinner that Birchfields was located not far from the site of the ruins of a medieval monastery, Garnet suggested that they take a picnic lunch out to the lovely meadow nearby. Naturally, when Evalee heard the plans under discussion, she demanded to go, too. So, of course, Scott, Kitty, and Cara must be included.

The monastery was some distance from Birchfields, up a little traveled country road. With such a large group, three vehicles were needed to make the trip. Garnet, Blythe, and Dru would take the open carriage, while Jeff, who must transport his portable easel and painting box, would drive Lenora, Lalage, and Neil in the landau. Since it was Miss McPherson's day off, Garnet had asked Faith to take the children with her in the pony cart.

Now Faith was watching as Jeff helped the Bondurant girls into the landau, noting how cool and pretty they both looked as they seated themselves and unfurled dainty, frilled parasols. Above the squabbling of the children about who would sit where, Faith could hear their amused laughter. They were probably laughing at something that Jeff had said. *He is certainly being his most charming self today*, she thought with chagrin.

She waited impatiently while the maids brought out two large wicker hampers containing the picnic food, and Martin, the footman, strapped them on the back of her mother's carriage. At that moment, Jeff and the Bondurants set out at a brisk pace, and Faith knew that the two couples would arrive at the lovely old monastery long before she could manage to get there. Still, she flicked the whip over the heads of the two fat, lazy ponies pulling the cart, hoping that they wouldn't lag too far behind.

The hillside where the old priory stood was covered with rough tussocks of grass and jutting rocks green with lichen, wild heather, and bracken. It looked for all the world like a stage setting for some medieval play or opera, Faith thought. As the curtain rises, the audience waits in anticipation for the entrance of the actors in the play. Would it be a drama, a farce, a comedy, or a tragedy?

Why am I so fanciful, always imagining? Why can't I just enjoy the day for what it is—a family outing? Faith asked herself irritably.

But as the day progressed, as if by some preordained script, she began to see yet another drama unfold. Coaxed into a game of dodgeball with the children, Faith saw Jeff and Lenora leave the others and make their way up the hillock to the stone ruins. A few minutes later, she saw him climb up onto one of the broken turrets and extend his hand to help Lenora up. Together they leaned on the ledge—Jeff, gesturing with animation; Lenora, listening as if entranced.

It's like watching a pantomime, Faith thought, with Jeff directing Lenora to take a graceful position against the ledge. Then, as if following his suggestion, Lenora lifted both hands to her hair and freed the waves of pale gold to tumble down on her shoulders. Jeff took her blue chiffon scarf, draped it loosely about her, then stepped back, his head to one side as if to check the effect. Apparently satisfied, he propped up his sketchbook and began to draw.

"Look out, Faith!" Scott Cameron's shout jerked her out of her fascinated trance as the ball whizzed by her head. She ducked just in time and, catching the ball, threw it at him with furious verve.

It was only sheer determination and willpower that kept Faith from looking again at the little scene being enacted on the hillside.

* * *

Garnet surveyed the setting with self-congratulatory approval. What a good idea it had been to picnic here. She had forgotten how peaceful and serene this place was, almost as if the peace that had prevailed here at the old monastery in days gone by had somehow blessed the whole area. Since she had only a very rudimentary knowledge of English history, the fact that bigotry, cruelty, and bloodshed had been perpetrated on this particular stretch of land did not invade her pleasure.

It was a beautiful day, and all her guests seemed to be enjoying themselves. Garnet's eyes roamed over the small groups. The children couldn't be happier. Rod and Blythe were wandering about, holding hands like two young lovers. Even Randall, his hat over his eyes against the bright sunshine, drowsed contentedly on the hillside with Dru beside him.

How charming Neil was being to Lalage Bondurant, Garnet thought, and his patience with her rather spoiled younger sister, Evalee, was admirable. Such a gentleman! Her glance darted over to Faith, hoping that she was taking note of Neil's considerate behavior. Garnet frowned. Faith had seemed so distracted lately. Did she mind that Jeff had asked Lenora to model for him? The thought crossed her mind, but it was time to set out the lunch, and she quickly dismissed it.

In spite of the lavish feast, Faith's usual healthy appetite failed her. She felt consumed, instead, with a raging jealousy that made it impossible to swallow. It lodged like an iron ball in her throat, weighting her chest and stomach. What made it worse was knowing the emotion was unworthy, yet she seemed incapable of setting it aside.

She knew all the reasons that she should not feel toward Lenora as she did. The object of her envy was not at all responsible for incurring it. No one could be sweeter, kinder, or more thoughtful than Lenora. She was so unaffected and unself-conscious, gracious to everyone.

It was Jeff who monopolized Lenora the entire long weekend he spent at Birchfields, but it was Lenora on whom Faith vented her suppressed fury. She could scarcely bear to be in the same room with the two of them, to see Jeff's eyes following the other girl's every movement, to hear him persuade her to pose for "just one more sketch," to suggest that they return to the site of the old monastery time and again.

"I want to get the details right, then I can fill in the background," he explained. "Once I do that and position the figure of Guinevere where I want it, I can work on the actual painting in my studio."

Since propriety would not allow Jeff and Lenora to go alone, they all had to pack up and go again to the picturesque meadow below the ruined priory, and Faith had to endure the agony of seeing Jeff spend another long day with Lenora.

Jeff was totally oblivious to the turmoil he was causing in Faith, and the fact that he was so indifferent to her suffering made it all the more acute. She tried to tell herself that he was an unfeeling brute, but she knew he was simply oblivious to everything but his project.

In her present distress, however, Faith could not separate

Guinevere from Lenora. They had become one in her mind, and she could not control her anguished envy of the time her cousin was spending with the man she loved. So she prayed earnestly to overcome her feelings.

For the first time, she understood Paul's words in Romans 7:15: "I do not understand—for what I want to do, I do not do, but what I hate, I do."

If Faith had only guessed the depth and seriousness of the secret correspondence between Lenora and Victor Ridgeway, some of her heartache would have been allayed. As it was, she had no idea that her cousin slipped downstairs early each morning to be the first to look over the morning post, to look for and almost always find an envelope in a dear and familiar handwriting, then to keep it hidden until she could read it privately. If Faith had known all this, her suffering over Jeff's seeming interest in Lenora would have been greatly reduced.

Still, although she despised the way she felt about Lenora, Faith could not help wishing that her cousin had never come to England. It was wrong, so wrong, she realized, and she deeply regretted her bitter troubled thoughts but could not deny them.

Once when Jeff was wheedled into a game of tag with the children, Faith took the opportunity to glance through his sketchbook. Her heart wrenched as she saw the exquisite sketches he had made of Lenora—so delicate, poetic, romantic. Even though the sketches idealized Lenora, Faith had to admit that they were some of Jeff's best work.

With an audible sigh, Faith closed the book and put it back near his paint box. But not before her mother had taken notice.

Garnet gave her daughter a long look. Something was definitely bothering Faith. The usual bloom was missing, the lovely mouth drooped, the eyes were shadowed. Garnet's mother's heart felt the pinch of anxiety. Was Faith hiding something? Something that was making her ill?

What could it be? Then Garnet felt an inner alert. Jeff. It must have something to do with Jeff Montrose. That was it, Garnet decided with sudden enlightenment—Jeff's obvious infatuation with Lenora Bondurant. How ironic, she thought, that the very thing that had brought her such relief was making her daughter miserable!

Garnet frowned as she watched her daughter move rapidly across the grass where they had been picnicking toward a little curved footbridge built over the stream that ran through the meadow. She saw her pause there for a moment to look down into the water, and wondered what Faith was thinking.

If she could have read Faith's mind, Garnet would have been quick to caution her against the decision she was making. Garnet could have told her of her own folly. In love with one man, she had recklessly pursued another to make her true love jealous.

But Faith was as strong-willed and stubborn as her mother had been under similar circumstances, and her frustration and anger blinded her to the perils of the course she had decided to take. *A little jealousy might be very good for Jeff*, she thought, and she was determined to give him a taste of his own medicine!

*   *   *

Faith's plan never had time to be put into operation. Her preoccupation with Jeff and Lenora had made her completely unaware of what was happening right under her nose. While she had been observing Jeff's constant posing and sketching Lenora for his proposed painting of Guinevere, another romance had been quietly blooming.

Therefore, it came as a total shock to Faith not a week after the picnic when Neil Blanding showed up unexpectedly one afternoon. From her bedroom window, Faith took note of his arrival and made quick work of tying up her hair with a new ribbon and putting on a fresh blouse, then ran down the stairs and out onto the terrace, where lemonade was being served.

"Where's Neil?" she asked casually.

"I think he went down to the lake," Lenora replied without moving, since Jeff was busy doing another sketch of her.

Plotting just how she would manage to take advantage of this fateful opportunity to flirt with Neil in plain view of Jeff, Faith did not see the two figures coming toward her up the path from the lake. When she heard Neil's voice hailing her, she lifted her head in surprise. *What luck!* she thought. When Lalage stopped to pick some flowers beside the trail, Neil walked on ahead.

He was smiling, and Faith felt a small tug of guilt when she realized how happy he seemed to see her. Maybe she'd been wrong not to value him more. Maybe Neil would be the right one for her, after all. He was such a dear, always so patient, so considerate. She *did* love him—in a way—

"Hello, Faith, we were just coming back up to the house. It's almost tea time, isn't it? The afternoon just seemed to slip away from us."

"Oh, Faith, hello!" Lally greeted her too, waving one hand holding the small bouquet she had just picked.

The smile on Faith's lips froze as Lally came up beside Neil and slipped her arm through his. Her left hand rested possessively on his sleeve. It was then that Faith saw on the third finger the gold ring bearing the Blanding heraldic crest—three roses encircled with laurel leaves—the same ring Neil had offered *her* at least twice in the past four years!

Faith looked from one to the other. Neil was gazing tenderly at Lalage, whose happiness was evident in the shining dark eyes.

146

Faith swallowed hard, taking it all in with mixed feelings of disbelief and then gratitude. At least she had been saved from making a bigger fool of herself than she might have. What if she had blundered stupidly into suggesting to Neil that they become engaged? And all just to spite Jeff?

Whatever this meant to her, Faith knew without doubt that these two had found something special, something that had so far eluded her. Ironically she thought of the Grace Comfort message Annie had read to her that morning: "When you pursue happiness, it eludes you, but when you least suspect, it may alight upon your shoulder."

Would the kind of happiness she saw in the faces of Neil and Lally ever be hers?

Somehow Faith found the presence of mind to congratulate them both with an enthusiasm that sounded genuine. Then, with the excuse that she had left something in the boat house, she rushed past them down to the lake. There she leaned against one of the birch trees, drawing in deep breaths of cooling air. Her face flamed at the thought of what she had almost done! At least she had been saved from that humiliation. Thank God!

When she finally stopped trembling, she splashed her hands and face with lake water, then started slowly back toward the house.

Just before she reached the garden, she saw Jeff and Lenora strolling along one of the gravel paths, his dark head bent to her satiny golden one. The two of them were evidently deep in intimate conversation. The sight was like a dagger plunged deep into her heart, twisting agonizingly. She could feel all hope draining out of her, leaving her more empty and forlorn than she had ever felt before.

chapter
20

AT TEA TIME, on the afternoon that Neil and Lally happily announced their intentions and received Dru's and Randall's blessing, Garnet seemed outwardly calm enough. But it was hard to tell, Faith thought. However, when everyone dispersed to bathe and dress for dinner, her mother stopped her at the foot of the staircase.

"May I see you for a few minutes, dear?"

Upstairs, Garnet led the way into her bedroom without a word and motioned for Faith to take the slipper chair opposite her dressing table bench. When she spoke, Garnet's voice was very low, controlled.

"How could you have let this happen, Faith?"

It was pointless to try to explain that her feelings for Neil had never been strong enough for marriage, and she refused to confide that she had almost made the irrevocable mistake of suggesting marriage to a man she did not really love! So she sat quietly and let her mother vent her frustration.

"How could you have let the most marriageable young bachelor in England slip through your fingers? *You* should be announcing your betrothal tonight! *You* should be wearing the Blanding ring on your finger! But no! You are wasting the best years of your life while all the other girls snatch away the best men!" Garnet made no secret that she was was bitterly disappointed, even incensed.

Finally Faith could take it no longer. "What do you want me to do, Mummy?" she said, rising and flinging out her hands in a helpless gesture. "Neil and Lalage are in love. They're perfect for each other, and we should both be very happy we brought them together!"

Back in her own room, Faith sat at her dressing table, stunned and shaken.

"Is something wrong, miss?" Annie asked anxiously when her mistress continued to sit like a stone statue, not even moving when the dinner gong sounded.

In the mirror, Faith could see her maid standing behind her, holding a fringed Spanish shawl in her hands. She hesitated, debating as to whether or not to go down to dinner. Knowing her absence would only raise all sorts of questions, she shook her head. "No, Annie, nothing."

Then without another word, Faith rose and, taking the lacy scarf, she flung it around her shoulders, lifted her chin defiantly, and went out the bedroom door.

Descending the broad staircase, she could hear the sound of voices coming from the drawing room where everyone was gathered. She wondered how she could possibly put on a convincing act, joining in with the wishes for the engaged couple, while wondering whether Lenora and Jeff would be next.

"But I *must*," she told herself firmly. Strangely enough, the quotation in Grace Comfort's column Annie had slipped into her mirror only yesterday came to mind:

> I hold it true, what e'er befall,
> I feel it when I sorrow most,

'Tis better to have loved and lost,
Than never to have loved at all.

Was it, was it *really* better to lose one's love than never to love at all? And would she ever know?

*   *   *

"When I planned this ball, I never intended it to be an engagement announcement party!" declared Garnet as her maid carefully pinned the fragile, filigreed ornament into her elaborately coifed hair. "That is, unless it had been for Miss Faith—" The words trailed away plaintively.

Myrna said nothing. In all the years that she had served Mrs. Devlin, she had learned discretion. When her mistress was upset about something, it was best not to comment for fear of adding proverbial fuel to the flame.

"Ah well, no use crying over spilt milk, I suppose." Garnet sighed and rose from her dressing table, picking up her lacquered fan and making a final adjustment of her ruffled décolletage.

"No, madam, no use at all," the maid murmured, handing Garnet her shawl.

At the head of the stairs, Garnet saw that Jeremy and Faith, who were to receive guests with her, were already waiting in the front hall. They were laughing about something, of all things! What could Faith find to laugh about tonight? Garnet wondered irritably. After all, most of the girls she had come out with were now safely married! And tonight's announcement would put "finis" to what was probably her best prospect and maybe even her last chance.

Garnet checked her morbid thoughts. Well, it was foolish to worry anymore about it now. *If Faith doesn't care, why should I?* she asked herself, picking up the train of her blue satin gown and starting down the steps.

Garnet's annoyance with her daughter quickly disappeared with her husband's admiring comment. "Elegant, my dear. You look elegant."

"Yes, Mummy, you look perfectly lovely, as usual," Faith agreed.

"So do you, darling." Garnet nodded at her daughter, thinking, *What a handsome young woman Faith is and what a shame that she has been wasting the best years of her life.* She allowed herself one last regretful sigh.

Through the open doors, Garnet caught a glimpse of the first carriage pulling up to the front of the house. With a flourish of her fan, she took her place beside Jeremy and arranged a cordial smile on her face. From her manner, no one would ever suspect that her mood was anything but euphoric.

For Faith, who had attended many such affairs as a debutante, the evening was all too familiar. It was as if she were an actress who had played the same role countless times in the same theater. Of course, with the added element of the announcement of Lalage's engagement to Neil, tonight was different, special. Although Garnet's parties were always spectacular, tonight she had outdone herself, hoping to please Neil's aristocratic relatives.

The loveliest flowers from the garden perfumed the air. The band brought from London filled the rooms with the most beautiful music—the lilting waltzes and popular melodies of the day. Yes, Garnet had planned everything perfectly, down to the last tiny detail. *Even to arranging a lovely luminous moon for the occasion*, thought Faith with a smile and a little sigh as she glanced out toward the terrace.

151

Why did a moon always make her feel somehow melancholy? Maybe because she most often gazed at it alone?

It was so ironic, Faith could not help thinking. Only a few years ago it was *her* engagement to Neil Blanding that her mother had expected to announce at such a festive party. Faith looked around the room and out toward the conservatory with its tropical plants and exotic flowers. Wasn't it in there at a ball very like this one that Neil had first proposed to *her*? She could still see Neil's handsome face, the puzzlement in his clear gray eyes.

"I don't understand, Faith, I thought you loved me—" he had begun.

"I'm sorry, Neil, I truly wish I could. It would all be so . . . pleasant and easy if it were possible. But it isn't. And it wouldn't be fair and honest to let you believe that it is."

"But, why? It *could* be possible if you'd only let it. We have so much in common. It could work—if you'd just try."

Faith had shaken her head, hating to hurt him. "But it wouldn't, even if I tried as hard as I could. The reason it can't is . . . because I love someone else. I can't help that and I can't change it."

It had been Jeff then and it was still Jeff, even now when all hope was gone. Jeff had made it obvious this summer that it was Lenora he cared about. In fact, he had seemed obsessed with her.

Faith's gaze moved around the room, watching the dancing couples. There she was now—ethereally beautiful and graceful, dancing with one of the half-dozen young men whom she had met and enchanted in the space of the evening. However, Lenora seemed a little distracted, Faith observed, as she kept looking over her partner's shoulder as if expecting someone—

Of course. She was watching for Jeff! Hoping he'd come. But Jeff had not arrived yet. Maybe he'd forgotten about tonight. It wouldn't be unusual. Sometimes, if he was painting, Jeff lost track of days at a time. He was putting the finishing touches on the Guinevere painting, he had told them the last weekend he'd been down. Then it would have to be carefully varnished before it was ready for exhibition.

Subconsciously, Faith began to tap her foot to the tune of a waltz. Out of the past came the memory of her first dance with Jeff—at his mother's wedding to Rod Cameron. At fifteen, she had been dizzy with delight that the tall, handsome young man had asked her to dance. Even then, Jeff was a superb dancer, twirling her skillfully about the ball-room. Later he had dutifully appeared at her debutante ball to claim a dance with the honoree, and on other occasions at Birchfields, they had moved together in rhythm to the music of her mother's hired musicians. Being in his arms, circling the floor time after time had been an oft-remembered dream. Hope had blazed in her then—a hope that had been dealt a fatal blow this summer.

Faith winced involuntarily, suddenly aware that her new shoes with their French heels were beginning to pinch, that she was tired of smiling, that it was getting late—and Jeff had still not come.

153

chapter
21

AFTER CONSULTATION, both families yielded to the couple's pleas to marry in the historic Jubilee year, and plans went forth without the usual long engagement period.

On the morning of Lalage's wedding, Faith awakened and lay still for a few minutes before the significance of this day crashed on her consciousness. A part of her wanted to pull the covers back over her head and escape into blessed nothingness, but she knew she had to face it, get through it somehow.

She had promised her mother that she would take the flowers down to the church. So, although it was still early, she dressed quickly and slipped down the stairs. Since no one else was about, she let herself out through the French doors of her mother's morning room and out into the glorious sunshine just beginning to stream through the trees.

Thousands of spider webs veiled the lawn sloping down from the terrace like a jeweled fairy net sparkling with the dew caught in each intricate thread. There was a freshness about the morning, the rare kind of summer day about which the English like to brag but seldom experience. Yet the misty sunshine promised clear skies—*a perfect day for a wedding*, she thought with a pang of regret.

As she approached, she saw that the sun falling on the ancient gray stones of the little church gave them a golden glow. Mounting the steps, she read the carved words on the arch over the door:

Enter this church and leave behind
All worldly woes, the cares that bind.
For here God reigns and Grace abides.

She turned the heavy twisted handle and went inside, then through the vestibule and into the sanctuary, where the faint odor of old polished wood and candle wax and the fragrance of faded flowers from the Sunday service still lingered.

Her arms full of daylilies and pink peonies, Faith walked up to the chancel rail and unhitched the gate to the altar. As she took the steps one at a time, her heart began to pound.

Suddenly reality receded, and her imagination filled the empty church with friends and family and turned her simple skirt and blouse into an ivory satin gown with a chapel train. She swayed a little, still holding the flowers, and closed her eyes.

She could see Jeff, splendid in a Prince Albert coat, with a boutonniere of white carnations in his lapel, standing to one side . . . waiting for her. She had only to take a few steps forward and they would be side by side.

Breathlessly she waited, her head turned toward the sacristy. Soon she saw the rector in his starched white surplice coming through the door. Opening the prayer book, he began the ceremony:

"Dearly beloved, we are gathered here today—" His resonant voice sounded just as it had the evening before at the rehearsal. Almost without thinking, Faith's lips began to move. Word for word, she repeated the vows, pausing to give

Jeff time to say his part. Then, when the minister asked for the ring . . . Faith's eyes popped open.

She felt dizzy and disoriented. What in the world was she doing? How wicked to pretend such a thing in this sacred place! Going through a mock ceremony with someone she loved who did not love her—

Faith jerked herself back from the make-believe world she had entered. Briskly she walked into the vestry and opened the cabinets to find vases for the flowers she had brought. Then she spotted the white wicker baskets that her mother must have sent over earlier for the bouquets that would be placed at the foot of the altar.

She turned on the spigots at the sink, filled the brass holders with water, and placed the flowers in them. Dru and her mother were coming from the house later to arrange them.

Empty-handed, she stood there for another minute, then shuddered. The dim interior seemed cool, almost cold, on this warm midsummer morning. Her hands were icy. It was as though the weight of all that had taken place within these ancient walls had suddenly descended upon her.

Faith hurried out from the vestry into the silent church echoing with the songs of a thousand hymns that had been sung here, the chords of organ music playing the triumphant Glorias and Hallelujahs, the dirges and wedding marches. Shivering, she came out into the bright sunshine, feeling the beauty of blue sky and soft air forcibly, almost like a physical blow.

Faith had believed that Jeff and she were somehow destined for each other, that eventually all her dreams would come true. Now, painfully, she began to realize that the heartbreaking truth of life is that many dreams die—

*   *   *

Annie came into Faith's room, looking flushed and a bit harried. The reason did not take long in coming out.

"Your mother says I'm to help Miss Lenora dress and Miss Evalee as well. Don't see why Nanny can't do it when I've got my hands full enough as 'tis."

"Well, if that's what Mummy wants, Annie, go on. I can get myself ready. Besides, everyone's eyes will be on the bride, not me," replied Faith indifferently.

Annie placed her hands on her hips. "You'll be the one comin' down the aisle first, won't you? I watched the rehearsal last night, you know. You're the first anyone will see, and I want you to make your mother proud, miss. I'm *your* maid, after all. Your mother and Mrs. Bondurant are both fussin' with Miss Lalage. And Miss Lenora doesn't really need me. It's that little magpie, Evalee. If you ask me, if someone doesn't settle her boots, she'll be a fair handful in no time at all!"

"Oh, she's just full of life and excited about her sister's getting married."

Annie said no more but pressed her lips together and went to the armoire. She took out the ice-blue satin bridesmaid's gown, its shimmering skirt making a slithering sound as she spread it over the taffeta coverlet.

"Oh, my, 'tis truly beautiful!" sighed Annie, fingering the wide royal blue sash that would be tied in bows and streamers down the back. Then she went back to the armoire and lifted down the romantically brimmed blue velvet Gainsborough hat and brought out the matching blue satin slippers.

"You'll be a picture, for sure, Miss Faith—the color's yours and the shape of the hat! La, but won't Mr. Jeff want to paint you in *this!*" she exclaimed.

157

The mention of Jeff struck Faith like a dart. If Jeff would want to paint any bridesmaid, it would be Lenora, not her. After the bride, it was Lenora, with her delicate beauty, who would be the focus of all eyes.

Annie turned to Faith and, seeing what was written on her face, admonished her. "Now, don't be lookin' like that! You should be smilin'! Just like Grace Comfort said in her piece today: 'A happy bridesmaid makes a happy bride'," she quoted.

"Oh, no, please, Annie. Not Grace Comfort again!" groaned Faith.

"You don't need to be scoffin'. She had a lovely piece in this mornin's paper. In fact, I put it on Miss Lalage's breakfast tray so she could read it herself. It's all about weddin's and brides and bein' in love," said Annie smugly. "You should be thinkin' more on those lines yourself, if you ask me, miss," she added with a little toss of her head. "Especially, now that you've let that nice Mr. Neil Blanding get away!"

"Oh, Annie, you're incorrigible!" Faith smiled.

"Well, whatever *that* means, miss, I'm sure," sniffed Annie. "You're not gettin' any younger, you know," she called over her shoulder as she left the room.

Faith had to laugh. Annie was right. She *wasn't* getting any younger, but that wasn't her real problem. *She* could dream all she wanted about weddings, but if the man she loved didn't share her dream, what good would it do?

*   *   *

A hushed air of anticipation hung over the little church as the observers waited for the bridal processional to begin. Garnet beside Jeremy, sitting in the pew behind the Bondurants, had a direct view of Druscilla. The look of complacent happiness on her face sent a splinter of envy and resentment through

Garnet. She immediately chided herself even as she told herself it was understandable. After all, it *should* be *her* daughter, not Dru's stepdaughter, getting married in this chapel today. And to Neil Blanding, too!

Garnet stirred restlessly and felt Jeremy's concerned glance. She smoothed her apricot silk skirt with nervous lace-mitted hands. It was really almost too much to bear. How could Faith have been so foolish as to turn down Neil time after time?

The first solemn bars of the Lohengrin wedding march resounded, filling the interior of the small building to the rafters. Garnet turned her head slowly as the slim figure of her daughter passed in the aisle beside her. Head held high, her piquant profile set off by the artistically dipped brim of the picture hat, Faith walked with stately grace, holding the bouquet of roses and lilies of the valley tied with blue satin ribbons.

Garnet's eyes followed Faith as she took her place on the bride's side of the chancel rail. What a waste! Garnet sighed. Faith could have had everything if she had accepted Neil's proposal—position, privilege, eventually probably a title. Now what was to become of her?

Faith stood watching Lenora come down the aisle with measured pace. How exquisite she was. No wonder Jeff had fallen in love with her. And where was Jeff, anyway? Everyone had expected him to arrive with the Ainsleys for the wedding, but he had not come. He had sent the excuse that he could not leave a work in progress, and Lydia further explained that he was rushing to meet the entry deadline for a painting he wanted to enter in the Waverly Exhibit. Strangely enough, Lenora had not seemed at all upset that Jeff had not appeared.

Faith was momentarily distracted from her thoughts by the sight of Evalee making the most of her role as flower girl.

Turning to the left and right, the little girl smiled at everyone, stopping every few seconds to toss handfuls of rose petals in the path of the bride.

Then Lalage appeared on Randall's arm, and Faith drew in her breath. Certainly it would be difficult to find a more beautiful bride. There had been frantic consultation as to where to find a suitable wedding gown on such short notice, and it was finally decided to alter one of the lovely evening gowns she had brought with her and not yet worn. Of white peau de soie, its off-shoulder bodice had been filled in with Brussels lace, and the same lace had been used to fashion stylish leg-of-mutton sleeves. Tiers of lace had been attached to form a cascading chapel train, and Lydia Ainsley had insisted that Lally borrow her own bridal veil.

In a few minutes the ceremony began, and Faith found her mind wandering, her eyes moving over the assembled guests, all listening intently to the minister's words and the bridal couple's responses. Suddenly Lydia Ainsley caught her eye and smiled, inclining her head slightly in acknowledgment. Faith smiled back, thinking how grateful she was for Lydia's friendship, her supportive strength, her inspiration.

Only recently when Faith had confided a sense of confusion about her future, Lydia had encouraged her. "When I've felt that way, I've gone to the Psalms—particularly chapter 37, verses 3 and 4."

Faith had quickly looked it up: "Trust in the Lord. . . . Delight thyself also in the Lord; and he shall give thee the desires of thine heart."

Would He *really*? Jeff was the secret desire of her heart. But now he seemed totally beyond her reach.

chapter
22

TWO DAYS after the wedding, every room downstairs was still
filled with reminders of the gala event. Huge arrangements of
garden flowers scented the atmosphere, and Evalee insisted on
wearing her flower girl dress and carrying the bridal bouquet
she had caught when Lally tossed it.

As for conversation, almost every comment centered
around the bridal pair and their future together. Dru
rhapsodized on the beauty of the bride, the gallant grace of
the groom. Blythe complimented Garnet on her superb
management of the entire affair, particularly in view of the
short time there had been to make preparations. Garnet
mentioned Lally's going-away costume of soft cream-colored
mulleton trimmed with passementerie and fringe. And the
adults had to agree with Evalee that the occasion had most
certainly been a *real* party.

At the end of the week, Blythe and Rod and their children
left for London, where they were to have a few days' visit
with Jeff before attending the opening of the exhibit at the
Waverly Gallery, which had accepted his painting, "Guinevere."

Having seen the departure of her summer playmates—
Scott, Kitty, and Cara—Evalee was everywhere at once. Still

stimulated by the excitement of the wedding, the child began making a nuisance of herself. Realizing that she was lonely and begging for attention, everyone tried to put up with her antics, but her persistence was irritating.

With Lalage on her honeymoon in Scotland, and Lenora strangely distracted, and with Miss McPherson's duties at an end, Faith gallantly took on the task of keeping Evalee occupied and out of mischief.

She led the little girl on an exploration of the estate, usually ending up down by the lake, where Evalee liked to wade and float the armada of toy sailboats left by the other children.

Although this amused Evalee for hours at a time, Faith's heart was sore. The lake held special memories of times with Jeff. Here they had spent hours talking, feeding the swans, skipping pebbles across the smooth surface, creating circles within circles. Everywhere she looked was a reminder of the emptiness in her own life, the hopelessness of her love for Jeff.

One of her most vivid memories, the one most precious to recall, was a special afternoon while Jeff was still at Oxford. He had brought his sketchbook down with him to the lake and had been idly doodling. After about an hour, he had thrown it down in disgust.

"I need instruction, Faith. I can't get past a certain point. I don't know enough about perspective or composition, and I don't have the basic tools I need to be an artist. And that's what I *really* want to do with my life! I know that sounds crazy—but it's the truth." He turned toward her with an air of desperation. "You're the only one I can be honest with, Faith. Rod is art-blind . . . just *try* to discuss the subject with him! And Mama doesn't *want* to hear!"

He had looked so unhappy, so discouraged, that Faith had impulsively put her hands on his shoulders and leaned her head against his.

"Oh, Jeff, I'm sorry. What can I do to help?"

"Believe in me, Faith, just that."

And then Jeff had kissed her. It was their first real kiss. In it were all of Faith's dreams, her expectations, her hopes. There had been something very moving in Jeff's plea—a need for her strength, her loyalty, and love.

"Don't ever stop, Faith—believing in me," he had said at last.

She had kissed him again, this time with a lingering sweetness.

"I promise I never will," she had whispered.

That had been the spring before he had made his decision, before he had had his near-religious experience about becoming a painter.

Did Jeff remember that scene? For Faith—that day, that kiss, those words were a treasured memory, cherished as a special bond between them of mutual trust and love. How could he have forgotten?

*　　*　　*

At lunch one day Dru read aloud from a letter from LaLage, postmarked Scotland:

Dearest Family,

We have just had the most heavenly day. We went to Tweedside in Abbotsford, Sir Walter Scott's estate. It is very grand, but sadly enough, turned out to be rather a "white elephant" for him as he went into great debt to build it, continually making additions until he had to spend the rest of his life writing books in a desperate attempt to avoid bankruptcy.

We also visited Melrose, about two and a half miles east of Abbotsford, to see the picturesque ruins of the monastery Scott used as background in his "Lay of the Last Minstrel." Our guide

163

told us that the heart of the Scots' hero-king, Robert the Bruce, is buried beneath the high altar. Isn't that the most romantic thing you've ever heard? But then Scotland is the most romantic place—or maybe any place would be romantic with Neil!

Dru looked around the table, beaming. "The child is deliriously happy! What a summer filled with romance this has been!"

Faith could not resist a glance at Lenora to see what her reaction to her sister's wedded bliss might be. Was she the least bit envious of her younger sister's happiness? But Lenora's expression was one of dreamy sweetness, and Faith felt a sharp dart of pain. Was she thinking of Jeff? Such a prospect caused Faith to feel more isolated than ever.

A few days later, Jonathan left to meet the Cameron family at the Claridge Hotel in London. He would be accompanying them to the Waverly opening before leaving for Boston and Cape Cod, where he would join Davida and the children.

Faith would have loved to go up for the opening, too, but she dreaded seeing in Jeff's painting, "Guinevere," what she feared most—that Jeff had fallen in love with his model. So she made plans to view it alone during the month-long showing.

She believed that Jeff had absorbed the pre-Raphaelite myth—that a woman should be a goddess, desirable but unattainable; that if she loved in return, she would be stepping down from her pedestal. Knowing that Jeff had patterned his technique after the artists he admired so much, she now believed he might have been tempted to embrace their values. If only she could share with him what she had discovered from her own research—that few of the pre-Raphaelites had formed lasting relationships, enduring marriages.

"Why doesn't he understand that loving and being loved is the most important thing in any life?" she anguished.

Fai'h knew that the Bondurants were waiting for Lalage and Neil to return from their honeymoon before leaving for their home in Charleston, South Carolina. The plans were to meet in London and go together to the Waverly Gallery to view Jeff's painting.

Observing Lenora during the days immediately after the wedding, Faith could not read her thoughts, but her cousin's dreamy expression was that of someone in love. Faith was consumed with curiosity. Had Jeff communicated with his Guinevere? She yearned to know but dared not ask.

On the evening following the opening, Jeremy announced at dinner that he had brought home some interesting news, and suggested they open one of the remaining bottles of wedding champagne.

Garnet lifted her eyebrows. "Are we celebrating something special?"

"Indeed, yes. Quite special, I should say!"

"Are we going to have another party?" piped up Evalee who, as the only child now in the house, was allowed to dine with the grown-ups.

"I think my news merits a party," agreed Jeremy jovially. "In fact, it probably calls for a *double* celebration."

"Why must you always create so much suspense, Jeremy?" demanded Garnet with a slight frown.

"My dear, *this* news deserves a proper anticipatory moment—" He unfurled the newspaper he had under his arm and held it up. "Jeff Montrose's painting, "Guinevere," has received an honorable mention at the Waverly exhibit and, I might add, rave reviews!"

Faith darted a quick look at Lenora, who paled then flushed pink, one delicate hand fluttering to her throat.

Jeremy continued. "Moreover, Waverly Gallery has issued the astonishing statement that his painting has been purchased by an anonymous buyer for an undisclosed amount. Apparently, the gallery spokesman 'leaked' the information to a reporter—" He studied the article again through the glasses perched on the end of his nose. "It is the highest sum ever paid for a painting by a new and hitherto unknown artist. However, he adds that from now on the work of young Geoffrey Montrose will be increasingly in demand!"

"Blythe must be elated," murmured Garnet, sending a worried glance in Faith's direction.

Faith was never sure how she got through the rest of the dinner hour. She had only a blurred recollection of toasts made, congratulatory comments, and excited predictions about Jeff's future. But the moment they retired to the drawing room, Faith excused herself and hurried upstairs.

By some inner direction, she found herself in the old schoolroom, the place of refuge she had often sought in times of childhood distress. Holding herself as if in physical pain, she curled up on the window seat and looked out at the gathering darkness.

She should be happy for Jeff, happy for his success, and that the love he felt for Lenora had been successfully transferred onto his canvas. It had resulted in a prize-winning painting, after all.

What did the Bible say about love? "Love seeketh not its own—" If she really loved Jeff—and she did—she knew she should share everything he must be feeling. Yet, all she could feel was a wrenching sense of loss and despair. Faith put her head down on her knees and sobbed.

Sometime later, Annie found her there and was dismayed when Faith turned a pale, tear-stained face toward her.

"Oh, my, miss, whatever is the matter? I went to turn down your bed and lay out your night clothes, and I waited for ever so long, but you didn't come. It's past midnight, miss—"

Faith pushed back her hair that had come loose from its pins, making no effort to check the tears that continued to roll down her cheeks.

"Oh, Annie, I'm so miserable!" she moaned.

Annie could not believe her eyes or her ears. To hear Miss Faith take on so! Was this the independent, steady young woman she had come to admire so much in the last five years since she had become her lady's maid? She thought she knew her mistress—thought they had become so close, closer than what Mrs. Devlin or, for that matter, her own mum would consider proper. She had seen Miss Faith at close range, and a more sensible person it would be hard to find, especially among the pampered gentry. Annie had her own opinion of them, having observed some of the shallow young women who attended house parties and such at Birchfields. But she was genuinely stricken by the look on her young mistress's face, the sadness in her voice.

Then she remembered the Grace Comfort piece she had clipped out of this morning's paper after Mr. Hadley, the butler, who was always addressed by the household staff and who always had first look at the paper when it was brought from the dining room, had finished with it. She had intended to send it to her younger sister Beth who, according to their mum, was walking out with Tim Givens, the butcher's helper in their village.

But now it seemed Miss Faith might need its wisdom more. So after only a second's hesitation, Annie whisked the creased newsprint out of her apron pocket and spoke briskly.

"Now listen to me, Miss Faith. You have more than most to be thankful for, I'm thinkin'. There's not a bit of use for you to be talkin' like that. Here's what the Good Book and Grace Comfort would say to you—" and Annie began to read aloud:

Weeping may endure for a night, but joy cometh in the morning. (Psalm 30:5)

No matter how dark the stormy night, dawn will surely come.

A dream is never dead, its sweetness will remain. And as an ancient Chinese proverb claims, If you keep a green bough in your heart, surely a singing bird will bring you joy again.

Wiping her eyes with the backs of her hands in a childlike gesture, Faith unfolded herself from the window seat. "You're right, Annie," she said to her earnest little maid. "I'm through crying now. And tomorrow, everything will look better—or, at least, different."

"Come along, then, miss. I'll fix you a nice cup of hot milk so you'll sleep well. You're just worn out, that's all, what with takin' over the charge of Miss Evalee, that little scamp! She's a right handful—anyone can see that!" Annie shook her head as she led the way out of the schoolroom with Faith following more slowly. "I suppose the Bondurants will be leavin' soon now that they've married off Miss Lalage." Turning, she gave Faith a sharp look. "It isn't that Mr. Neil Blanding you're cryin' over, now is it?"

"No, Annie," replied Faith, wondering why the girl had not guessed that it was Jeff who was the source of all her pain . . . and all her happiness.

chapter
23

TRUE TO HER word, Faith tried to rise above the lurking sense of melancholy that continued to plague her. And the very next day something happened to lift the spirits of everyone in the household who had been experiencing the let-down so common after weeks of wedding planning.

On Monday evening her father, looking enormously pleased with himself, called another impromptu family meeting to make yet another announcement.

"I have a nice surprise for you."

"For goodness sake, Jeremy, don't keep us in suspense *again!*" Garnet exclaimed, adding dryly, "On the other hand, I think we've had our share of surprises lately. I'm not sure I could stand another."

"I think you'll share my delight in *this* one, my dear," said her husband with confidence. "I am expecting a guest this weekend."

"There's nothing surprising about that! We have guests almost every weekend."

"Yes, I know, but this is a very special one." Jeremy paused as all eyes focused upon him, then said triumphantly, "*Grace Comfort* will be here this Friday evening!"

He waited a minute for the effect of his dramatic announcement, which was not long in coming.

"*Grace Comfort?*" echoed Garnet and Faith in unison.

The others at the table looked on in bewilderment.

"Yes, indeed. Grace Comfort. And I cannot tell you what a feather in my cap this is!" Jeremy continued. "We must all do our best to roll out the red carpet, extend the royal treatment. If I can get Grace Comfort to sign a contract— Well, my dear," he said, turning to Garnet, "what was that set of sables you had your heart set on? They're yours if all goes well."

"Who, may I ask, is Grace Comfort?" Randall wanted to know.

"Yes, who in the world is she?" asked Dru.

"You wouldn't believe it if he told you." Garnet rolled her eyes. "She writes the most sickening treacle for the newspapers—"

"Now, wait a minute, dear," Jeremy interrupted. "Of course, the poetry is atrocious. And maybe Keats, Shelley, Barrett, and Browning—whom Grace quotes frequently— should be turning over in their graves! But this writer is immensely popular. The people at the newspapers tell me they receive more letters addressed to Grace Comfort than to any other columnist. Readers are constantly writing in for reprints of one or another of her columns. Why, I'm told that her 'Moments of Inspiration' column sells more copies of the daily paper than the headlines!"

He turned to Randall for confirmation, as if he, a man, would surely understand the business side of things. "My firm feels that landing Grace Comfort as one of our authors would be a tremendous coup, with endless possibilities for spin-offs—collections of some of her best columns, gift books for all occasions. Our editorial staff has already come up with dozens of ideas for capitalizing on Grace Comfort's immense popularity."

"Then I suppose you want me to ready the room overlooking the garden for the illustrious Miss Comfort," said Garnet, with only a trace of sarcasm.

"Wait until I tell Annie!" Faith said.

"*Don't!*" Garnet held up her hands in alarm. "If the maids find out who's coming, they won't be fit for anything!" Turning to Dru, she explained, "*They* all worship this Grace Comfort and think she's the personification of the Oracle at Delphi!"

"Everyone reads Grace Comfort, it seems, from the Queen to our own kitchen maid," declared Jeremy. "She has found a way to touch every heart in some incomprehensible way, whether it is to strike a chord of memory or pathos or nostalgia. Sometimes for a childhood one has never experienced, a love that one has never known— Still, there is that indefinable . . . *connection* . . . she seems to make with all her readers. They recognize a kindred soul, I think, though they probably couldn't put it into words."

"Well, personally, I can't wait to meet her!" laughed Dru.

*   *   *

By midweek, some of Garnet's friends with visiting grandchildren invited Evalee over to spend the day, leaving the ladies with a rare day of leisure. Garnet suggested that she and Dru go to a china shop specializing in Wedgewood to select a tea set for Lalage. Faith gratefully seized the opportunity for a free afternoon and caught an early train to London.

At the station she took a cab straight to the Waverly Gallery. At last she would see Jeff's "Guinevere."

At this time of day the gallery was not crowded, and Faith was allowed to wander alone through the rooms, making an unhurried circuit of the exhibit. Then, from an archway into a smaller, well-lighted alcove, she saw Jeff's painting, and her heart gave a little leap of recognition. Slowly she moved forward and stood before it.

All Faith knew about art was what she had derived from Jeff and the books she had read, trying to understand the nuances and subtleties of some of the paintings he admired. But *this* she knew instinctively was *good*.

She might not know about the technicalities of brush strokes, perspective, or composition, but she saw that Jeff had succeeded in bringing a mythical figure to life. Everything about Guinevere was luminous—the skin tones, the sheen of the hair, the texture of the clothing, the glimmer of the finely detailed jewelry she wore. More than that, the expression of love, longing, and loss in her face spoke to Faith's own heart.

She did not know how long she stood in a trance-like state in front of the painting. It pulled her into the time and place that Jeff had created through his skill—a time of romance, mystery, mysticism.

Oh, Jeff, you are an artist. It has all happened for you just as you dreamed.

On the way home, Faith stared unseeing at the landscape past which the train rattled and rocked. The image of the painting was imprinted on her mind's eye. Today she had found out what she needed to know—first, that Jeff's dreams had come true and, second, that he loved Lenora.

*   *   *

On Friday afternoon Lenora walked alone in the garden. Her mood was both sad and hopeful. Sad, because the weekly letter she had looked for in this morning's mail had not come. She had written to Victor, telling him of the Bondurants' plans to do some sightseeing in London, where they would be staying at the Claridge Hotel until Lalage and Neil returned from their honeymoon. Lenora suggested that Victor call on her there.

With her time in England growing short, Lenora feared that he might not act on this information. For some reason she could not fathom, Victor seemed to feel that his love for her was hopeless. He had hinted of some secret obstacle that would keep them forever apart. What had he meant? Didn't he know how much she loved him? She *must* convince him before it was too late.

Lenora turned out of the boxwood maze and took the path down to the lake. Beautifully peaceful, it had become one of her favorite places to stroll. She loved to sit on the mossy bank and watch the graceful swans glide over the surface. Here she would take out the latest of Victor's love notes and re-read it, each one more precious than the one before.

She had almost reached the place where the broken branch of a willow tree provided her a seat when she heard footsteps on the gravel path behind her and turned her head to look over her shoulder.

"Victor!" she gasped. "What on earth are you doing here?"

He came toward her, both hands extended, looking at her with such tenderness and love that Lenora's heart melted.

"I know this may come as a shock, but I've been invited for the weekend," he told her, smiling.

"But I never thought—Uncle Jeremy didn't tell me—"

"I *know*."

"What do you mean? How could you know?"

"Please, my darling Lenora, listen to me before you say another word."

Lenora looked at him through her haze. "Uncle Jeremy only said he was expecting a—a guest for the weekend—"

"It must come as a surprise—"

"I only knew Uncle Jeremy had invited a prospective author, and I—I guess I thought *she* would be the only one."

"Listen to me, darling. Hear me out," Victor pleaded. "Why do you think Jeremy Devlin—your uncle—invited me down here this weekend?"

Puzzled by his question, Lenora asked some of her own. "Because he knew we had all become friends on board ship? Or has he known you from before? I do recall seeing the two of you talking together the day he met us at the ship—"

Victor shook his head vigorously.

"No, no! English gentlemen—or even transplanted Americans—quickly learn that a man's home is his castle. He doesn't invite just anyone—a casual acquaintance—into it—especially not to a place like Birchfields and especially not *this* particular summer, when it was the scene of a family reunion." Victor spoke decisively. "Now, I will tell you the *real* reason I'm here.

"Jeremy Devlin hopes his firm can acquire me as one of their authors. I am a writer—oh, don't look impressed—I'm no literary giant. I am what is called a 'popular writer' or perhaps even, in some inner circles of the literati, a 'hack.' You see, Lenora, I write under a pseudonym. If you were a reader of the London tabloid journals, you would recognize the name immediately."

He reached for Lenora's hands, brought them both to his lips, kissed them, then clasped them tightly as he looked deep into her eyes.

"Remember, on board ship, that last night when I told you I had a secret, something I wasn't sure you'd understand? Well, the fact is, my darling, *I* am 'Grace Comfort'."

He waited for some kind of reaction, but none came, so he continued his explanation.

"Years ago, when I first became a reporter for the

newspaper, Grace Comfort's column was written by an elderly lady in the country, who sent in her weekly 'Moments of Inspiration' from her Cotswold cottage. Unfortunately, when the old lady passed away, the column stopped, much to the dismay or, I should say, the outrage of her readers. Well, my managing editor got the idea that someone else should pick up the column and continue writing it, so I, as an eager young reporter, volunteered. I studied some of the past columns she had written, copied the style, and started writing, thinking it merely a stepping stone to my goal of becoming a real journalist. Well, as it turned out, I eventually *became* Grace Comfort permanently.

"These papers are read mainly by housemaids and chars— the common people of England, looked down upon by the upper classes. It may even dignify what I do to call it 'inspirational poetry.' Sometimes it isn't even poetry—just a kind of hodge-podge of thoughts gleaned from other sources and put into some rather simple, sentimental verse." He paused to study her reaction before he continued.

"Yes, my darling, *I* am Grace Comfort." Victor smiled. "And 'Grace' is quite successful. She receives tons of fan mail, with requests for reprints of her little biweekly column. I turn them out rather easily now after all these years and . . . to be vulgar about it . . . I have made a great deal of money."

Still Lenora made no comment.

"Jeremy Devlin wants to collect my best columns and put them in book form—you know, the sort of gift book people buy for their grandmothers and maiden aunts—*Words of Inspiration by Grace Comfort*. The publishers know that a book like that will sell a million copies!"

When he seemed to have run out of words at last, Lenora broke her long silence.

"But, Victor, you must do an enormous amount of good

with your verses. If people love them so much—they must love you, too! I don't care what you say or who you say you are—I think I know you well, and I know you must write things that help people, give them hope and strength—"

"And 'comfort'?" Victor gave a self-deprecating little laugh. "The more I write this sort of thing, Lenora, the more uncomfortable I am with the whole thing. I borrow from the great writers of all time, then capsulize and sugarcoat their words for the masses—"

"Don't put yourself down," she scolded. "When it comes right down to it, how many people do you know who read Socrates and Plato or, for that matter, Baudelaire or Thomas Carlyle? You are probably inspiring and helping more people in a week than any of those so-called 'great' writers have done in a lifetime."

"You are very dear—" began Victor doubtfully. "What concerns me is that when your parents find out *who* I am, they may not consider me worthy to ask for their daughter's hand in marriage—"

Lenora drew in her breath, her eyes glistening with sudden happy tears.

"Oh, Victor, you honor me by asking, but I don't think we need fear what my parents will say." She paused, then said shyly, "I am of age. I'm twenty-two, so I don't need their permission, but I know I'll have their approval and blessing. The important thing is that we love each other."

"Oh, my dear Lenora—"

She took his hand. "Let's not tell anyone until after your meeting with Uncle Jeremy. In the meantime, I'll have a chance to talk to Drucie, my stepmother. Then we'll go together to see my father."

When he still looked doubtful, Lenora spoke up. "Oh, Victor, I'm sure everything is going to work out!" She

176

laughed lightheartedly. "Isn't that what Grace Comfort would say?"

A mischievous smile lightened Victor's serious expression and his eyes filled with merriment as he lapsed into a cockney accent. "If thet h'aint the truf—and wot's more, there's no use borrowin' trouble as me dear auld mum wuz fond to sigh! Not to crost thet bridge 'til we comes to it. We'll jest 'ope fer the best!"

Part V
The End and the Beginning

Home to America
September 1897

More things are wrought by prayer than this world dreams of.
—Alfred Lord Tennyson

chapter
24

BIRCHFIELDS was strangely quiet. The guests had dispersed in all directions—the Camerons, to Ireland; the Bondurants, on their way home to America; Faith's parents, to Scotland. Faith herself had been included in the invitation to the Etheridges' hunting lodge but had declined, resisting all her mother's repeated urgings to accompany them.

"I'm not good company just now," Faith had told her, and with this, Garnet had to reluctantly agree.

"But I don't like the idea of your staying here alone," her mother fretted.

"I won't be alone. Annie will be here, and so will the rest of the staff," Faith reminded her. "And I'll have Bounty to ride. I'll be perfectly fine, really. Besides, after all the company we've had all summer, a little aloneness suits me perfectly."

Taking Faith at her word, the Devlins had gone off to the Highlands with two trunks, Garnet's assorted luggage, and Jeremy's elaborate fishing gear.

For the first few days, Faith relished the solitude. It was a relief not to have to pretend constantly, avoiding her mother's worried looks, her anxious questions, spoken or unspoken. But by the end of the week, Faith's naturally outgoing personality found the silence and the solitary meals beginning to pall.

Sensing a subtle change in the weather—the early-morning chill, a scattering of golden leaves—Faith felt a keen restlessness one morning as she walked in the garden. The aromatic odor of bonfires filled the air with a pungent scent and added to an indefinable aura of melancholy. P1 She was reminded of a painting she had once viewed with Jeff, "Autumn Leaves" by Millais. The painter had depicted four sorrowful-eyed young girls, their expressions sad, as if mourning the lost summer. Where *had* the summer gone? Could it be September already?

Feeling lonely, she decided that the best remedy might be to take a long walk into the village and do a few errands.

The autumn sun drowsed over the village, strangely quiet at midday, with all the children at school, the men at work in field or factory, the women about their housewifely chores after the morning's shopping. Faith finished her few errands and started back for Birchfields, disappointed that her outing had not lifted her spirits much.

* * *

In London, Jonathan took affectionate leave of the Bondurants in the lobby of the Claridge Hotel. His earlier parting with his young half-brother, Jeff, had been particularly poignant. Jonathan regretted the fact that the young artist's preoccupation with his painting had made it impossible for the two of them to become better acquainted, as had been his hope in coming to England.

Consequently, he had not learned anything more about the unresolved constraint between Jeff and his mother, Blythe, over the Montclair heritage. Perhaps in time it could all be settled, Jonathan thought as he boarded the hansom cab the hotel doorman had secured to drive him to the dock. Maybe it would have been better if Dru had deeded Montclair to Jeff instead of to him anyway. At least, Davida would have been happier.

Having traveled more lightly than most gentlemen, Jonathan's baggage was soon under the supervision of a porter, who was wheeling the cart toward the steamship to be loaded. Jonathan checked his ticket and passport, then looked up and about him at the busy ship's terminal. It was then that he saw something that startled him.

Could it *be*? he asked himself.

Not ten feet away stood a young woman dressed in a simple but stylish blue traveling ensemble and wearing a smart hat on which a small feathered bird perched in a nest of velvet ribbons. He recognized her immediately. Impulsively, he moved forward to greet her.

"Miss McPherson!"

She turned and, for an instant, registered a look that Jonathan could not analyze. Shock? Pleasure? Or had her clear eyes really widened in—fear?

"Why, Mr. Montrose," she returned in a husky voice.

Almost as tall as he, her gaze was level with his, and Jonathan saw her for the first time apart from her role as the children's nanny at Birchfields. Her face—the high cheekbones, a sprinkle of golden freckles across the bridge of her small straight nose, those clear gray eyes now showing unguarded emotion—suddenly seemed, if not beautiful, at least intensely interesting and attractive.

"Whatever are you doing here?" he asked.

"I'm on my way to America," she replied, gesturing toward the three girls standing nearby. "I'm traveling companion to the Ellender children—Margaret, Edith, and Louisa. They're going to live with their grandmother in Westbridge, Massachusetts."

183

"Then we'll be fellow passengers." Jonathan beamed his pleasure at the prospect. "I'm sailing on the *Medea*, too."

Her expression underwent a subtle change.

"Well, perhaps not, Mr. Montrose. We are booked second class, and so I doubt very much if our paths will cross often, if at all."

Suddenly Jonathan experienced a coolness in her tone that implied her reluctance to continue their acquaintance. Was it her Scottish reserve that seemed to cancel the friendly rapport they had enjoyed this summer at Birchfields, or was it something more subtle he detected in her attitude?

"And, of course, I shall be quite busy with my charges," she added, placing one hand on the shoulder of the smallest child, who moved closer at her touch.

Jonathan took his cue. "Yes, of course." Then, as an afterthought, his curiosity got the better of his judgment, and he asked, "Do you plan to stay long in the States, or will you be returning to England after you deliver your charges?"

A slow flush suffused Phoebe's face. "I'm not quite sure. I was given my return ticket. However, as long as I'm there, I thought I might investigate employment opportunities."

Jonathan nodded and tipped his hat. "Well, it was a pleasure to see you again, Miss McPherson. I wish you the best."

As he turned away, Jonathan had a moment of regret. He would have enjoyed the delightful Miss McPherson's company on the ten-day ocean voyage. *Too much?* came some inner cautionary query. Perhaps. Straightening his shoulders and resisting an impulse to turn back and lift his hand in a farewell salute, he mounted the gangplank and was directed to his quarters in the first class section.

If he had looked back, he might have seen the pensiveness in the clear gray eyes taking note of his departure.

chapter
25

The Claridge Hotel
London, England

WHY in the world should I feel so nervous? Blythe asked herself, noticing her hands were shaking as she fastened on the pearl choker Rod had given her for their first anniversary. She knew the answer, of course. She always felt tense before an encounter between her husband and her son.

But things should be very different now, she argued with herself. The animosity, the angry scenes, and yes, she had to admit it, the jealousy between them should be a thing of the past. In spite of Rod's opposition, Jeff had pursued his dream and—best of all—had succeeded in fulfilling it. Couldn't Rod accept that, accept Jeff as an individual with his own life plan?

Blythe's heart swelled with pride at the thought of her son's sudden fame, the recognition of his peers and critics alike. For a moment she closed her eyes, feeling the sting of happy tears.

In her memory she could see Jeff as a small boy, the lamplight on the library table at Avalon shining on his curly dark head, his hand clutching a pencil, busy on the paper before him. She saw herself sitting in a chair nearby, reading or embroidering, assuming in her complacency that Jeff was doing his homework. Blythe smiled in retrospect, remembering how often she would find that he had been drawing instead of doing his sums.

His pictures, crude as they were, showed a tremendous imagination even then—knights in full armor; horses, if indeed out of proportion, with necks too thick and legs too long, were at least recognizable. She remembered also coming across pages of heraldic shields copied painstakingly from books Jeff had inherited from Corin Prescott, their neighbor in Kentburne, England, where she and Jeff had lived for the first ten years of his life. Interested in the ancient families of Britain and the feudal system, Corin had introduced Jeff to them.

Blythe had simply accepted Jeff's early scribblings as a childish pastime and had never taken it seriously, or at least had never imagined he would choose it for a career.

Blythe would never forget receiving Jeff's letter telling them that instead of using the passage money they had sent him to come to Virginia for the summer, he was using it for a vagabond odyssey to France, Spain, and Italy. There he would visit the great museums and study the old masters because—and this was the greatest shock of all—he planned to study painting!

Remembering how angry Rod had been that day, Blythe shuddered. In fact, she had never seen him so angry before or since.

Taking a last appraising look in her mirror, Blythe decided she would go down to the lobby to wait for Jeff. Perhaps they would have a chance to talk before Rod and the children joined them. After a summer of freedom to roam the vast estate at Birchfields, the children had felt confined in their hotel room and had grown restless, and Rod had taken them to the park.

This would give her some time alone with Jeff. Yes, that would be a good idea, Blythe thought, picking up her gloves and satin handbag and preparing to leave the suite. She would tactfully suggest that Jeff refrain from any kind of debate with Rod in this brief time they would all be together.

*　　*　　*

Upon entering the spacious lobby of the Claridge, Jeff saw his mother before she saw him and paused for a minute to admire her. *She is really quite beautiful*, he thought, seeing her objectively and with an artistic eye.

She was wearing purple and wearing it with flair, something few auburn-haired women could do. But her complexion and dark eyes, inherited from her Spanish mother, complemented her rich-hued hair. In fact, Jeff thought, she bore a striking resemblance to the the wife of Edward, the Prince of Wales—lovely Princess Alexandra, whose beauty and style were so often praised in the British press.

At the same moment he was admiring his mother, she turned suddenly and spotted him, and with a graceful wave of one gloved hand, started toward him.

"Darling, how wonderful to see you!" Blythe said, reaching up to kiss her tall son's cheek and checking the urge to brush back the stubborn lock of dark hair that fell forward on his brow.

She took his hand and led him to one of the small sofas in a windowed alcove on the far side of the lobby, then seated herself and patted the plump cushion beside her.

"We'll have a few minutes by ourselves before Rod brings the children back from the park," she told him. "Time for a nice, cozy chat."

Jeff had to smile at his mother's choice of words, groping mentally for just what they might mean. He rather suspected her "chat" would be a thinly veiled "suggestion" that he be properly deferential and respectful to his stepfather.

He regarded her indulgently. Not too long ago, Jeff might have rebuffed any such efforts on her part to restrain him from expressing an opinion that might clash with Rod's. Then he would have felt it necessary to assert himself and say something outlandish just to prove his independence.

Jeff recognized a maturity in himself now that made that kind of response unnecessary. A hard-won self-confidence, to be sure, but a validation that gave him a comfortable reassurance that he was his own man. Rod no longer intimidated him.

As it turned out, the coveted private chat was soon interrupted by the sight of Rod's towering figure striding through the hotel entrance with the children. As soon as Scott saw Jeff, he broke into a run and flung himself enthusiastically at him. The little boy had formed a strong attachment for his older half brother during the summer. The little girls were bubbling over with excitement, their words tumbling over one another.

"Mama, Mama, we saw the Queen!"

"She went right by us in her carriage!"

"We saw her! We saw her! Truly!"

"People said that Princess Beatrice was with her!"

Over the twins' heads, Blythe looked inquiringly at Rod. "Really?"

He smiled and nodded. "Yes, indeed, everyone in London seems to recognize the royal carriage on sight, and everyone crowded to the edge of the street, lining up to get a glimpse of Her Majesty," he said casually.

"You really saw her? What does she look like?" asked Blythe, trying to imagine the reigning monarch on parade.

"Well, actually, I couldn't see her all that well," Rod admitted with a shrug. "All I saw was the flutter of a black-gloved hand and some movement beyond the carriage window. It was the comments of people around us that gave me most of my information."

"Oh, now, Papa, don't tease! It really *was* the Queen, Mama," Kitty assured Blythe.

"Wouldn't Evalee be pea green with envy if she knew that *we* had seen the Queen and *she* hadn't?" said Cara smugly.

"Now, Carmella, don't be unkind," admonished Blythe automatically as she reached out to straighten her daughter's ruffled collar.

Jeff had risen to his feet and his eyes met Rod's. There was a split-second as they mutually took stock, then Jeff thrust out his hand, and his stepfather took it in a strong grasp.

"I believe that congratulations are in order," Rod said in a gruff voice.

"Thank you, sir," Jeff acknowledged. Then, looking down at the twins, his voice assumed a tone of mock astonishment. "And who are these pretty, grown-up-looking ladies!"

The little girls giggled and squirmed and preened themselves under Jeff's teasing scrutiny.

They do *look adorable*, Blythe thought with understandable pleasure. All her children were handsome, but the twins were certainly unique—alike and yet remarkably different, with the same copper curls, the same heavily lashed brown eyes, except that Kitty's were soft and warm, while Cara's flashed with fire. They were dressed identically in white French lawn dresses. Only their hair ribbons were different—Kitty's blue, Cara's red.

"Well, shall we all go in for a celebration before we visit the

189

Gallery again to see Jeff's painting?" Blythe suggested. She got to her feet, putting one hand through her son's arm and the other through the one that Rod offered.

When they parted a few hours later, Rod extended an invitation to Jeff that he knew in advance would be turned down. The boy had no interest in accompanying them to Dublin for the horse show. But he was pleased to see the new maturity in his son, and their farewell was amiable.

Then Blythe kissed Jeff good-bye. "I hope we'll see you in Virginia before too long, darling."

Jeff gave her a vague reply but thought to himself, *Maybe sooner than you think, Mother dear. Maybe sooner than you think.*

* * *

As soon as he had seen his family off, Jeff went directly to Victoria Station and took the next train down to Birchfields. All the way, thinking of the last enigmatic conversation with Faith, he argued with himself. After all the heady publicity about the "Guinevere" painting, he had been too excited to catch the subtle undertones of that conversation. Too much press, too many questions . . . and of course, with all the reporters surrounding a celebrity like Victor Ridgeway, who had turned out to be "Grace Comfort"!

Jeff shook his head. Who would ever have thought it? And the announcement that Ridgeway had been the "anonymous buyer" of his painting because it reminded him of his fiancee, had compounded the shock. This, followed by Ridgeway's engagement to Lenora, had taken everyone by surprise and increased the madness.

No matter, thought Jeff. The painting had received more notice than it ever would have otherwise, with himself the beneficiary. Not that the critics had not been extraordinarily kind and generous—

Two recent articles by notable critics had appeared in two separate art magazines. One had praised his "technique, his style, reminiscent of the best of the pre-Raphaelites." The other had compared his work favorably with that of Millais and Burne-Jones.

Jeff had almost memorized the article in *Art World*, and the words ran through his mind now:

The entry of the painting by Geoffrey Montrose, "Guinevere," far outshone any of the others by new artists. Although some may have thought it imitative of the pre-Raphaelites with their allegorical themes and medieval romanticism, Montrose's rendition of the legendary beloved of King Arthur has a freshness, an originality that is unique, for he has given us the ideal of nineteenth century beauty.

Certainly none can gainsay the technical skill of the artist. The brushstrokes, the exquisite rendition of fabric, hair, skin tones is well done. And his background of the castle, painted as if a prison for the Queen, shines with an aura of particular mystical beauty. He has also caught the subtle sadness of expression on Guinevere's face that tells us of her inner conflict between loyalty and love.

I can say only "Bravo!" The artist's prize is well deserved, and I feel we can expect further outstanding work from young Geoffrey Montrose.

Recalling the praise from a difficult critic, Jeff's spirits soared again. This was his breakthrough. How many artists had such luck? So many struggled for years in poverty and obscurity without attracting any attention at all. And he had been prepared to do that, too, determined to do whatever it took to become recognized as an artist.

But Lenora had changed all that. Lenora, who had walked down the terrace steps at Birchfields and into his life. He had recognized her instantly—his "Guinevere." He owed her a lot—more than he could ever repay—

And now thanks to this incredible stroke of luck—well, talent *and* luck—he at last dared speak what was in his heart. He could not wait to share all this with Faith.

How loyal she had always been. Believed in him, encouraged him, supported his dreams. Her steadfast enthusiasm for his talent had never wavered. She had never faltered in her belief that one day he would be a famous artist. Now he had fulfilled that faith. Suddenly Jeff realized how much he had missed being with Faith this summer, how much he needed her. Impatiently, he willed the train to go faster.

chapter
26

LEAVING the village, Faith took a secret path through the woods. She and Jeff had discovered it years ago, and she followed it now until it emerged just above the graveyard at one side of the small stone church.

The vanishing sun had left slowly, trailing gold streaks among the dark, gathering clouds. As Faith passed the little cemetery where she and Jeff had sometimes wandered, reading the markers, she felt a weird sense of unreality in the strange light of approaching autumn dusk. How short a time ago all that seemed. *How quickly life goes by, leaving youth and hopes and dreams behind,* she thought. She shivered and hurried on.

"Don't be so morbid!" she told herself aloud. "What would Grace Comfort say?" *Grace Comfort, indeed!* She laughed at her own foolishness.

Thinking of the revelation of the popular columnist's real identity, followed by the even more startling revelation that Lenora and Victor Ridgeway had been carrying on a secret romance for months was mind-boggling. Their private wedding had taken place in a small church in London, with only the immediate family present. In fact, no announcement had been made until the couple was safely en route to Italy for their honeymoon.

Faith drew in a deep breath. It had been a summer of surprises, she thought, a season of weddings and happy brides. Except for me. And Jeff. He must be heartbroken.

Feeling chilled, she picked up her pace. What would happen now? Jeff would probably take off for some remote place to heal his wounds and paint his heart out. But what was to become of *her*? What direction would her life take now? By all standards of society, a young woman who had been "out" for three seasons should be married by now or, at the very least, engaged. According to her mother, she had let one opportunity after the other slip by. Faith was sure that her mother despaired of her ever making a good match.

So what now? For such a long time Faith had believed that her destiny was intertwined with Jeff's. Now that must be put behind. The "Guinevere" painting, if nothing else, had convinced her of that.

But Faith still firmly believed that God had a purpose and plan for her life. If not love and marriage—and she still felt if she could not have Jeff, there could never be anyone else—then there was some other path He wanted her to take. It was up to her to pray until she found it, even if it meant being alone and lonely for the rest of her life. It didn't matter. All that mattered now was finding what God had planned for her.

As she left the main road, the golden afternoon was quickly evaporating in the cold, clammy mist rising from the river. Suppressing a shudder, Faith turned into the gates of Birchfields.

The wind rose, scattering the vari-colored leaves over the garden now bereft of most of its color. Then she saw one single golden rose—*summer's last glorious gift*, she thought. She paused for a moment to bend down and inhale its deep fragrance. It seemed somehow a symbol of hope, a talisman of courage, a sign that she should take heart.

Walking up the driveway toward the house, her step was lighter. Suddenly she was startled to see a tall, familiar figure, pacing impatiently on the stone terrace. It was Jeff! Her heart hammered.

Seeing her, Jeff began to wave his hands. Then he broke into a dead run. "Faith, Faith!"

In the fading light, his face seemed different somehow. Illuminated by the last brilliant rays of the dying sun, his complexion took on a golden cast, molding his features with new strength, bringing a new depth to his eyes.

"Oh, Faith, I've so much to tell you that I don't know where to begin. Just wait until you hear my plans!" He was grinning, his eyes sparkling, and he put his hands on Faith's shoulders, as much to steady himself as to get her attention. "You see, because of "Guinevere," the Waverly Gallery will take all the paintings I can do! Isn't that marvelous? Isn't it crazy!"

Faith tried to say something, but Jeff rushed on. "I've enough money to last at least a year while I build up my inventory of paintings. But the main thing is that I don't want to stay there anyway. London's no place to inspire the kind of paintings I want to do." His eyes blazed with new intensity. "I want to go to Virginia and live at Avalon! I know I can paint there!"

So Jeff had come to say good-bye. Faith closed her eyes, steeling herself to be brave all over again.

"So, what I'm really getting at is this—will you marry me, Faith? We'll have to do it right away. But that's no problem . . . we can get a special license. I know I'm rushing you, but I had to be sure of my future before I could ask."

Faith could not believe what she was hearing. "Wh—what are you saying, Jeff?"

"Well, I couldn't possibly have asked you to live with me in my shabby studio digs, but you have no idea how beautiful it is at Avalon—the island, the house, the woods. Oh, Faith, I can't wait to show you everything! And I'll paint wonderful paintings, and we'll be happy for the rest of our lives! It's what I've always dreamed, Faith—you and me at Avalon!" He put his arms around her waist and swung her around, hugging her hard before he set her back down on her feet. Then he stopped, suddenly serious. "You *will*, won't you? Marry me and come live with me in Virginia?"

"But, Jeff!" she protested when she had caught her breath. "You haven't even said that you love me."

He looked at her blankly for a second. "But of course I love you, Faith. Didn't you know that? But how could you help knowing? I've *always* loved you."

"But you never said—you never told me—" She turned away from him. "Why didn't you say something . . . before now?"

"I didn't think it was necessary. I thought it was understood. It was always understood between us—" He turned her back around to face him. "Or . . . at least I *thought* it was."

He drew her toward him and, under his touch, she felt a slow weakening of limbs and resistance. If this were all a dream—well, she would enjoy it while it lasted. Capturing her chin with one hand, he tilted her face upward until they were looking into each other's eyes. For a moment they stood as still as one of the garden statues. Then his lips found hers and Jeff was kissing her, and Faith knew it was not a dream, but *all* the dreams of her lifetime come true.

Gradually the doubts and heartaches of the last few months disappeared. Jeff loved her! Jeff loved *her!*

At length he released her, spun her around, and gave a jubilant "Hurrah!"

"We've all sorts of plans to make," Jeff told her as they walked together, arms around each other, into the house. "I took the risk of ordering our steamship tickets. All we have to do is pick them up. We'll be married right away. I don't want the fuss of a wedding, do you?"

Again he did not wait for Faith's reply but rushed on impetuously. "We'll spend our honeymoon in Virginia. You've never seen anything as spectacular as Virginia in the fall—"

Faith was in a complete daze, therefore the minor details of her marriage, the trip to America, the rest of her life with Jeff fell on deaf ears. All she really knew was that Jeff loved her and that there would never be anyone else for her. Whatever came, she loved him now and always.

* * *

It was raining hard when the hack they had hired from the small village train station drew up in front of the cottage loaned to them by one of Jeff's friends. Making a run for it through the gate of the picket fence and up the crooked flagstone path to the door, Faith felt the hood of her cape slip back and the rain whipping her hair into her eyes and against her wet cheeks.

Once inside, she stood huddled in the entry, the door behind her open to the wind-driven rain while Jeff paid the driver and pulled the baggage from inside the cab.

Suddenly the enormity of what they had done struck Faith and she began to shiver uncontrollably. The last twenty-four hours had passed in a blur of unreality.

Only yesterday afternoon she had been at Birchfields. Events had moved swiftly since then. With a wide-eyed

197

Annie's help, Faith had packed two suitcases while Jeff waited impatiently downstairs.

"Whatever will your mother and father say, Miss Faith?" Annie had asked over and over as Faith ran back and forth from armoire to dresser, pulling out clothes, emptying drawers, piling things on the bed for Annie to place neatly inside the suitcases.

"I hope they'll be happy for us, Annie!"

"But why not wait and tell them and have a proper weddin'?" the maid demanded, shaking her head disapprovingly. "Your mum will be *so* disappointed—"

"She's put on *two* weddings already this summer. I should think she'd be grateful not to have to do it again," declared Faith, laughing almost hysterically.

"But her *own daughter's* weddin' would be different, surely."

Faith stopped her frantic pace for a minute and turned to her little maid.

"Oh, Annie, stop fussing, please, and be glad for me! Don't you realize I am getting my heart's desire—the secret petitions of my soul?" Faith flung out her hands dramatically. "If I don't go now with Jeff—maybe—well, just maybe I won't have another chance. Don't you see?" She paused. "Maybe it would be better to do things differently. But I can't take that chance. Please say that you understand."

Annie pursed her mouth and folded her arms. "It isn't my place to say, miss, but—"

"Well, then don't say it, Annie. Please! Don't spoil this for me." Faith hurriedly put the last few items in her suitcase, closed the lid, and snapped the lock.

Now as she stood in the cold draft coming in the cottage door, Faith recalled that scene in her bedroom the day before and felt a deep, shuddering regret. Of course, she would have loved a wedding like Lalage Bondurant's in the little stone church where she had worshiped most of her life. She could see it now—sunlight slanting through the arched windows, flowers from her mother's garden banked in front of the altar, herself in her mother's heirloom lace veil—

But it wasn't to be so—not if she were to have Jeff. And there had been no contest, no debate in her heart about that. Even so, the brief, unsentimental marriage ceremony—if you could call it that—in the drab registry office had been rather bleak. That is, it would have been bleak without Jeff's firm handclasp, his confident smile.

On the train into London, she *had* timidly proposed that perhaps the Ainsleys should be told and invited to come with them, but Jeff had quickly countered her idea by saying Lydia would probably try to talk them out of their plans.

"We *could* change our sailing date," she had even suggested.

"No, Faith, one thing would lead to another, and we'd be stuck here for another month or more while everyone else got into the act. Your mother would insist on a big wedding and a reception with hundreds of guests. No. It's not as though we were children, after all—we're both of age and we don't have to ask anyone's permission for what we want to do."

Faith had never thought about it like that. She had always gone along with her parents' wishes. But Jeff was right about her mother. Garnet *would* have wanted to take over, change, and rearrange everything—

Just then, Jeff came running up the path and into the cottage with a great stomping of his wet boots, shaking his thick, curly hair out of his eyes, and setting down their luggage.

"What did you pack in yours—the family silver?" he joked. Then, seeing that she was shivering, he gave her a bear hug. "You're chilled, aren't you, my poor darling? I'll see if I can

199

get a fire going," he said and disappeared into the small parlor.

Faith followed, still shivering, her dampened cloak held tight around her.

Outside, the rain pattered steadily. The little cottage seemed dark and somehow unwelcoming. What were they doing here? Maybe, they should have gone to a hotel in London and spent the three days before their sailing date in luxurious surroundings, enjoying a *real* honeymoon—

But Jeff had told her he was taking her to a fairy-tale cottage in the woods—well, St. John's Woods—

"You'll love it, Faith! It's just your imaginative cup of tea." He had laughed. "We'll be like Hansel and Gretel—snug and cozy in our wee cottage in the big woods."

But Faith was already having second thoughts about the wisdom of what they'd done. Perhaps instead of behaving as adults, as Jeff asserted they were doing, they were acting like runaway children.

Faith took a step farther into the center room and looked around. The fireplace before which Jeff squatted, using bellows to start a fire, was wide and of cobbled stone, and there was a rough-hewn wooden mantel displaying a framed motto cross-stitched in Olde English letters: *God Will Provyde.*

This message cheered Faith somewhat. Maybe God really would provide for them. Hadn't He brought them this far?

As the fire caught and flared into flame, some of the gloom disappeared. The flickering light threw a soft gleam on the mellow wood of the furniture, the faded chintz of the pillowed sofa and chairs. Faith moved closer to the hearth, and Jeff put his arm around her and pulled her close.

Gradually the dampness lessened and, warmed by the excitement of their elopement and their love, they began to laugh and joke in the old familiar ways.

*   *   *

In Scotland, Garnet stood at the window of the Etheridges' lodge, staring out at the rolling mists and waiting for Jeremy's return from his day's fishing. At rare intervals the sun broke through, sending myriad sparkles on the river beyond and turning the wild purple heather on the hillside into glistening amethyst.

Unmindful of the wild beauty of the scenery, Garnet's hands twisted, pleating the telegram she was holding. What was keeping Jeremy?

She saw him at last, his unmistakable figure clad in a rough Scottish tweed jacket and plaid beaked cap, carrying his creel over one shoulder and his fishing rod in his hand. From the satisfaction on his wind-burned face, Garnet knew he had had a good day's catch.

But his expression changed as soon as he came into the room and saw her.

"What is it, darling?" he asked. "Has something happened?"

She held out the telegram.

"Read it for yourself." The paper fluttered out of Garnet's numb fingers. "Faith and Jeff have eloped."

Jeremy put down his rod carefully and, shrugging off the strap of his creel, placed it on the tile hearth, then bent and picked up the crumpled yellow paper. His eyes moved over it, then he spoke gently.

"Well, my dear, they are in love—have been for a long time. Anyone could see that—that is if they had looked." There was an implied reproach in his words.

"But she could have made such a brilliant marriage—" Garnet's voice broke. "Or she could at least have had a beautiful wedding—" She pounded one small clenched fist into her open palm. "Oh, that foolish child! Married! And to Jeff Montrose, of all people! He's so immature, so irresponsible—"

"Garnet, don't upset yourself so. What's done is done. There's nothing you can do about it now," Jeremy said soothingly. "What matters is that our daughter has the man she adores. Yes, of course, they're young, but they have all their lives ahead of them—years to be wise, responsible, and mature. We should be happy that Faith is getting her heart's desire. Jeff has always been her knight in shining armor, you know. Wish them happiness, give them your blessing, dear."

"Blythe and Malcolm's son," Garnet said almost to herself. "How ironic."

Once she had deeply resented Blythe, the woman who had robbed Garnet of her own heart's desire—having Malcolm, whom *she* had loved most of her life. She had lost him twice—once to Rose Meredith and then again to Blythe, the beautiful young girl from California.

How was it that none of *her* dreams had ever come true? Why had she not received *her* heart's desire?

Then Jeremy's low voice broke into her thoughts.

"My dear, my very dear—" He held out his arms.

With only a slight hesitation, Garnet went into them gratefully, realizing that perhaps, after all, she *had*.

*   *   *

On the morning before they were to sail, Faith awakened before Jeff. She slid out of bed quietly so as not to disturb him, pulled on her robe, and tiptoed out to the tiny kitchen. She stirred up the ashes from the fire they had banked the night before, then filled the kettle and put it on to boil, feeling very "wifely" in this small domestic act.

The rain had stopped during the night, and a pale sun was struggling valiantly to push through heavy gray clouds, still hovering overhead.

Faith peered through the criss-crossed windowpane and looked out on what must once have been a pretty garden leading out into a small orchard. In spring, the gnarled apple trees were surely smothered in pink blossoms.

Subconsciously, a yearning sprang up within her to stay in this snug little country hideaway, do all the simple, homey things a place like this required. One of the two rooms upstairs could be converted into a studio for Jeff, and she could bring the garden back with flowers and grow vegetables and—

The hissing of the kettle announcing that the water had come to a boil snapped Faith back from her daydreams as she felt strong arms go around her waist and Jeff's rough cheek brush against her own.

"Good morning, my early bird," he whispered in her ear. "You shouldn't have let me sleep in. This is the day our great adventure begins!"

With these words Faith realized with a certain sadness that Jeff did not share her wish to remain in this little world apart they had fashioned for themselves for the last three idyllic days. He was excited and eager to be on their way to a new life.

Within hours, they found themselves in the frenzied hustle of the dock, getting ready to board the giant ship that would take them across the Atlantic to America, to Virginia.

While Jeff went to see about a porter for their trunk, Faith, heart pumping wildly, took in the scene surging about her. This was it. Here was the moment of departure—no turning back, no change of mind. Whatever qualms of conscience or doubts she had must be put behind her now.

In her heart of hearts, Faith knew Jeff was all the things her mother accused him of being—impulsive, reckless, irresponsible. But he was also compassionate, sensitive, talented, and had a firm belief that he was following a divinely decreed goal for his life. And what's more, he loved her—needed her.

Then there was no more time. Jeff was back, and his excited anticipation was contagious. She could feel it pulsating through her entire being. Holding his arm, she mounted the gangplank as he pushed a way for them through the other passengers crowding to the railing.

The huge ship began to move slowly, irrevocably out of the harbor. Faith watched the grayish water churn away from the hull. The figures on the dock waving good-byes became smaller and fainter.

A pang of the finality of it all struck Faith. Suddenly she recalled a painting in an exhibit Jeff had once taken her to see. The painting, entitled "The Last of England," was by one of the later pre-Raphaelite artists, Ford Madox Brown. In it, a young couple sat in the prow of a boat, presumably a tender, taking passengers to board a ship. Everything Faith was feeling—fear, hesitation, sadness, hope—was reflected in the face of the woman as she gazed on her homeland for the last time.

Jeff's arm tightened around Faith, and she looked up at him, love for him swelling her heart, tightening her throat.

Oh, God, Faith prayed, *Help us as we begin this journey.*

And the reassurance came, flowing into her mind from the book of Joshua: "I will not fail thee nor forsake thee. . . . Be strong and of a good courage; be not afraid, neither be thou dismayed: for the Lord thy God is with thee wherever thou goest."

Family Tree

In Scotland

Brothers Gavin and Rowan Montrose, descendants of the chieftain of the Clan Graham, came to Virginia to take possession of an original King's Grant of two thousand acres along the James River. They began to clear, plant, and build upon it.

In 1722 Gavin's son, Kenneth Montrose, brought his bride, Clair Fraser, from Scotland, and they settled in Williamsburg while their plantation house—"Montclair"—was being built. They had three children: sons Kenneth and Duncan, and daughter Janet.

In England
The Barnwell Family

George Barnwell first married Winifred Ainsley, and they had two sons: George and William. Barnwell later married a widow, Alice Cary, who had a daughter, Eleanora.

Eleanora married Norbert Marsh (widower with son, Simon), and they had a daughter, Noramary.

In Virginia

Since the oldest son inherits, George Bramwell's younger son, William, came to Virginia, settled in Williamsburg, and started a shipping and importing business.

William married Elizabeth Dean, and they had four daughters: Winnie, Laura, Kate, and Sally. William and Elizabeth adopted Noramary when she was sent to Virginia at twelve years of age.

Kenneth Montrose married Clair Fraser. They had three children: Cameron, Rowan, and Alan.

Cameron Montrose married Larabeth Whitaker, and they had one son, Graham. Later Cameron married Arden Sherwood, and they remained childless.

After the death of his first wife (Luelle Hayes), Graham Montrose married Avril Dumont. Although they had no children of their own, they adopted his nephew, Clayborn Montrose.

The Montrose Family

Clayborn Montrose married Sara Leighton, and they had three sons: Malcolm, who married Rose Meredith; Bryson (Bryce), who married Garnet Cameron; and Leighton (Lee), who married Dove Arundel. Bryce and Lee were killed in the War-Between-the-States. Clayborn and Sara's daughters-in-law were Rose Meredith (widow of Malcolm) who left one son, Jonathan; Dove Arundel (widowed, with one daughter, Druscilla); and Garnet Cameron (widow of Bryce Montrose), who remarried, this time to Jeremy Devlin.

Jonathan Montrose, son of Rose (Meredith) and Malcolm—was reared in Massachusetts by Rose's brother, John Meredith, and his wife, Frances. Jeff Montrose was Malcolm's son by his second wife, Blythe (Dorman).

The Cameron Family

Douglas Cameron married Katherine Maitland. They had twin sons, Roderick and Steward, and one daughter, Garnet. Stewart was killed in the war.

Faith Devlin was daughter of Garnet (Cameron-Montrose) and Jeremy Devlin, Garnet's second husband.

The Brides of Montclair Series

. . . is a sweeping saga of a single American family, from before the Revolutionary War to the twentieth century. The thirteen volumes are:

1. *Valiant Bride*
"If you enjoy reading romances, you'll enjoy reading *Valiant Bride*"—*Jane Mouttet, book reviewer, KHAC radio*

2. *Ransomed Bride*
"Earns a rousing A+"—*The Bookshelf WBRG*

3. *Fortune's Bride*
"Excellent . . . another triumph for Jane Peart!"—*Christian Readers Review*

4. *Folly's Bride*
This is the stunning "prequel" to Jane Peart's Civil War epic, *Yankee Bride/Rebel Bride*.

5. *Yankee Bride/Rebel Bride: Montclair Divided*
This novel is a newly revised expansion of the book that won the 1985 *Romantic Times* Award for Best Historical Fiction.

6. *Gallant Bride*
"Such a splendid book!"—a reader in Ontario, Canada

7. *Shadow Bride*
A continuation of the story of Blythe Dorman (many readers' favorite Jane Peart heroine) and her struggle to find lasting happiness.

8. *Destiny's Bride*
Druscilla Montrose finds love unexpectedly among the sun-drenched hills of nineteenth-century Italy.

9. *Jubilee Bride*
A Cameron and Montrose family reunion amid all the joy and romance of Victorian England.

10. *Mirror Bride*
Twins—alike yet not alike—search for their hearts' desires. (Due June 1993.)

11. *Hero's Bride*
A novel of epic faith and endurance during World War I. (Due June 1993.)

12. *Senator's Bride*
Love, politics, and abiding faith in this "between-the-wars." (Due spring 1994.)

13. *Montclair Homecoming*
The final volume of the Brides of Montclair Series, in which the last secret of the Montrose family saga is revealed. (Due autumn 1994.)